THE MISSING GIRL

SUMMER PRESCOTT

S. PRESCOTT THRILLERS

CHAPTER ONE

Curled up in a culvert to catch a few hours of sleep, Susannah made certain that she didn't move a muscle as the spider skittered down her cheek, tickling its way toward her chin. Once it had ventured far enough, its finely-haired leg exploring the corner of her lips, she darted her tongue out and brought it into her mouth, relishing the scrabbling of its legs as she crunched it between her teeth. One could never have enough protein.

The nation's most heinous female serial killer was on the run, after brutally neutralizing the unfortunate sheriff's deputy who'd been assigned to babysit her. Susannah regretted that she hadn't had time to revel in the thrill of power which never failed to consume her when she ended a life. She also mourned the fact that the only souvenir she'd been able to take with her was a hastily sliced, leaf-shaped piece of the female deputy's scalp, hacked off with a box cutter that she'd found in the deputy's desk. The sheer sloppiness of it all disgusted her, but she didn't have time for niceties. Wrapping the attached, dark, silken hair around the leaf of skin to keep the blood from soaking into the pocket of her jeans, Susannah had grabbed money from the deputy's wallet, as well as a cookie and a slug of cold coffee from the dead woman's desk, and headed out the door, the smell of rich, coppery blood singing in her nostrils.

Thankful for the cover of darkness, Susannah had run fast and far from the site of her captivity, hoping to put as much distance as possible between herself and the scene of her latest crime. She'd have to establish a new identity eventually, and plans for her new life had tumbled and whirled through her fevered brain as she slipped through the night with the grace and power of a predatory creature.

She wasn't impulsive generally, preferring to plot out, in glorious detail, the demise of those whom she deemed deserving of a horrifying death, but the elimination of the deputy had been necessary for her freedom. She'd simply had no choice. Now, she had to deal with the consequences of choosing a life on the run.

Dampness seeped through the seat of her loose-fitting men's jeans and the back of her yellowed thermal shirt, both of which had been stolen from a clothesline along the way. She remained motionless and prone, her stomach growling impatiently. The spider hadn't exactly been a treasure trove of nutrition, but Susannah couldn't afford to concern herself with such insignificant annoyances as hunger at the moment. Listening carefully to make certain that there were no cars approaching, she rose to continue her quest. She didn't know what she was going to do with him when she found him, but somewhere out there in the darkness, her estranged husband Tim moved and breathed and lived his life, without her. For now.

The sun dipped low in the sky, casting long shadows over the ditch, which reeked of rotted grasses and stagnant water. Susannah had spent the day sleeping, preferring to travel at night. Her caution had served her well, and so far, she'd managed to make her way deep into Iowa farm country. She was headed southeast, toward Chicago, figuring that her husband would most likely flee from their small town in Minnesota, rather than staying to face the whispers and stares which inevitably must have grown from the breaking news of his wife's peculiar hobby. Susannah didn't know, as yet, whether she wanted to linger in the embrace of her mild-mannered Tim, or kill him, but the relentless drive to find him gnawed at her with every step she took.

Chicago was her destination of choice for several reasons. First, and most practically, the city boasted several restaurants in which a chef of her caliber could make a decent living, while she plotted out her plan to find her husband. It was easy to disappear in large cities, remaining nothing more than a generic face in the crowd, and this particular Midwestern metropolis was notorious for having the country's highest percentage of unsolved murders. There were estimated to be more than a dozen serial killers skulking around the city's dark alleys and abandoned buildings, and while Susannah didn't relish the thought of competition in her craft, she knew that the odds of being able to commit murder and get away with it were pretty good. She found the prospect tantalizing.

Timothy Eckels, the socially inept mortician, whom she'd met in cadaver class, was the only man that she'd ever met who looked at her without judgment. He was the only human with whom she'd actually had what passed for a relationship. It would be a shame if she ended up having to kill him now that he knew what she was. She likely wouldn't have to make that decision any time soon, finding him would take time, and the possibilities available in Chicago would allow her plenty of time to figure out her next move.

Her joints popping as she stretched and crawled out of the culvert, Susannah glanced to and fro, squinting into the dying light to make certain that she could slip out of the ditch undetected. The area was remote. She'd only heard a handful of cars pass by the entire time that she'd been hidden, so chances of an encounter were slim. Once she was satisfied that no souls were about, she started off at a light jog, enjoying the humid chill of an early fall Iowa evening, staying ever alert for signs of life. She only occasionally heard the distinctive roar of an engine, or saw the points of headlights in the distance, and each time, was fortunate enough to have rows of corn, hay bales, or an aging barn to hide behind, until her fellow humans had passed.

There had been a horse in the barn that she'd hidden behind, and the poor creature whickered nervously the entire time she crouched on the other side of the wall, almost as if it knew it was in the presence of true evil.

The killer had learned by experience that it helped to be strong and have stamina when subduing a difficult victim, so Susannah had kept up a fairly rigorous fitness regimen for years now, a fact which served her well in her present circumstance. She jogged for several miles before stopping to rest alongside a small pond, conveniently located roughly a few hundred yards or so from the country road along which she'd been traveling. The darkness was getting thicker, but in the waning light, she barely detected the outline of what was undoubtedly a barn cat perched on a rock at the pond's edge, its tongue flicking in and out of the water.

"Good enough for you, good enough for me," Susannah commented, kneeling down several yards from the cat and dipping her cupped hands into the water for a drink.

The water tasted earthy, and there was far too much particulate matter in it, but she drank anyway, knowing that she wouldn't get far if she allowed herself to become dehydrated.

When she'd had her fill, and her heart had resumed its normal rate, Susannah stood and stretched, placing her hands in the small of her back. Turning toward the dirt road next to the pond, she froze when she heard the crunch of tires on gravel and saw headlights swing onto the road in the distance, heading her way. Ducking down into a crouch, adrenaline flowing, she slipped into a clump of tall grasses at the water's edge, mud and water sucking at her shoes and creeping up to her ankles. She cursed to herself when she heard the pickup truck approaching the pond, and her eyes darted about, searching for a weapon. The lumbering vehicle came to a stop, much too close for comfort. Frustrated that she'd been caught entirely unprepared for a murder, her mind raced.

At least the beams of the truck's headlights hadn't swept over her hiding place. Laying low would be her smartest option until whoever it was moved on, and hopefully that was sooner rather than later. Her knees and ankles quickly grew stiff from remaining motionless in a squatting position, and the long, coarse grasses surrounding the pond had made tiny cuts on her hands and face, which now itched abominably. Something in the muddy water slithered against her foot and Susannah bit the inside of her cheek, pushing away all reptilian thoughts so that she wouldn't run screaming into the darkness. Even serial killers had their phobias. Teeth grinding in anger at the interruption, she willed the driver to turn around and go away. Though she didn't particularly want to resort to drastic measures, she was more than capable, if it came to that. Her neck and shoulder muscles began to throb with tension, her dark anger toward the unwitting soul, who was impeding her progress, growing by the second.

Susannah's heart nearly stopped when the driver killed the engine, switched off the headlights and opened the pickup's heavy door. The metallic creak of it shattered the silence of the night, causing the stray cat to bound away from the water's edge. A pair of heavy work boots hit the loosely packed gravel with an audible thump, and Susannah didn't move a muscle. The boots scuffed slowly toward her hiding spot, then stopped. It took an extreme amount of self-control to moderate her breathing when her chest wanted to heave with murderous rage. She heard the distinctive rasp of a zipper and curled her lip in disgust when she heard a stream of piss splattering on the gravel, way too close to where she was crouched. She fully realized that, while the moon wasn't full, once the man had relieved himself, his eyes might have grown accustomed to the darkness well enough to see her among the grasses.

How could she kill him? Should she spring into action now, while he was vulnerable? She dared not even move enough to glance upward to determine how big he was, so the risk of taking the offensive was tremendous. The smell of urine assaulted her nostrils and she resorted to breathing through her mouth, thinking dark and bloody thoughts. After what seemed like years, the man zipped up, and instead of heading back into his vehicle, rustled his hands around in his pockets. Had he seen her? Was he reaching for a knife, or some other weapon? Susannah braced herself. If he made any move in her direction, she'd have no choice but to try to catch him by surprise. She'd aim for his eyes and other tender parts and hope for the best.

Her joints and muscles screaming from lack of movement, she heard a tap-tap-tap sound, followed by a quick scraping sound, which seemed familiar, but which she couldn't place until she smelled the distinctive tang of a newly-lit cigarette. The longer he stayed out in the dark, the better he'd be able to see. Her position was becoming more compromised by the minute. The man stood smoking, breathing in and out, seeming to be in no particular hurry. She resented every breath and ached to stop the effortless rise and fall of the man's chest. Susannah needed to know what she was up against, so she risked moving her head ever so slightly, to take a look at her potential adversary.

She needn't have worried. The man was absorbed in the tiny, glowing screen of his phone while he smoked. She could practically stand up and wave her arms and he wouldn't be able to see her. Since the man, who was rather large, it turned out, but in a squishy, overfed sort of way, was entirely distracted, Susannah considered killing him just because he'd stressed her out. She contemplated the sheer thrill of popping up and scaring the daylights out of him, but at that moment, he clicked his phone off, flicked his cigarette butt onto the gravel in a shower of sparks, and turned to climb back into his truck.

"Smart move," she thought to herself, with more than a tinge of disappointment.

Though she wouldn't mind killing the unwanted visitor, she didn't have time, and she needed to focus. He hadn't been part of the plan. She didn't want to have a trail of bodies following her wherever she went. That wasn't smart, it wasn't prudent, and more importantly, it wasn't her style. Susannah was tired of all of the maintenance killing that she'd had to do lately. There was no joy in it for her.

Murder was an art form in many ways for Susannah. There was a sheer, thrilling beauty in the sense of control that she felt, watching the life force ebb from the fear-darkened eyes of her deserving victims. Then, there was the practical side of murder as art – the souvenirs. She'd made stunning sculptures from the bones, skin and hair of her victims, gravitating particularly toward tattoos. She'd mourned the loss of her treasures when she had to leave them behind, in the cozy little house that she'd shared with Tim. Her creations were proof to her that even those who were of little worth, while still breathing, could be beautiful in their absence of animation. Susannah eagerly anticipated being in a position where she could revel in the creation of her art, and the thought of it sent a thrill, which felt searingly sexual, through her.

Once the fat smoker with the now-empty bladder had moved on, Susannah knew that she needed to travel faster in order to regain the precious moments lost squatting in the weeds. Slogging through the mud and muck, which now tainted her shoes and socks with the stench of decay, she made her way back to dry ground, stopping to rinse her shoes, as best she could, at the water's edge. The cat that she had seen originally had taken refuge behind a clump of brush, and watched her closely, the tip of its tail flicking back and forth.

CHAPTER TWO

Timothy Eckels stood, dazed, watching as the sheriff's deputies emptied the basement hideaway that had housed his wife's dark hobby. Evidence bags were filled with clumps of hair, carefully dried bones and leaves made of skin, as well as perfectly preserved tattoos, which had been stretched and touched up to be more colorful. He'd known that his quiet, mysterious wife, a chef by profession, had been a talented artist. What he hadn't even suspected, until very recently, was that murder and its relics had been her medium. The sheriff spoke from behind his shoulder, startling him.

"I gotta tell ya, Eckels...I find it awfully hard to believe that all of this," he gestured to the parade of evidence going out the door, "was happening right under your nose, in your own house, and you knew nothing about it."

"We kept to ourselves. It was her space. She didn't want me there," Tim replied simply, and without emotion.

"How could you have been living with a homicidal maniac and not known it?" the sheriff challenged.

"Are we going to have this conversation yet again?" Tim's eyes narrowed.

His wife had been a cold-blooded killer, and he was the one being treated with suspicion.

"We'll have this conversation as many times as we need to until I'm satisfied that you ain't lying. Is that clear?" the sheriff hitched up his belt, asserting his position in a way that Tim found most distasteful. Almost as distasteful as his grammar.

He was spared from answering by the sudden appearance of a deputy in the doorway, who seemed very concerned.

"Sheriff, we got a problem," the deputy announced.

The sheriff strode toward the deputy and inclined his head toward him, listening intently for a few minutes. He turned with a grim look on his face and rushed toward Tim.

"That bitch of yours escaped. Killed an officer to get out. Where would she go? You tell me how to find her right now," he demanded, the words hissing past his teeth.

"I don't know...we led very different lives," Tim shook his head, the color draining from his face.

His heart skipped a beat and his system flooded with adrenaline. His flight response made it nearly impossible to stand, stock-still, watching evidence techs shuffling in and out of the humble home. The sheriff was so close that Tim could feel his breath.

"You better have more for me than that," he growled, his voice low.

"I obviously didn't know her at all," Tim murmured, staring at a Tech who had bagged the contents of Susannah's night stand and was taking the bundle to the plain white van parked at the curb.

"Sheriff, we're heading over there now to join the manhunt," the deputy called out.

"I'm watching you, Eckels," the sheriff promised, his hand on his weapon as he strode toward the door.

The threat didn't faze Tim. He wasn't worried about the attempted intimidation by a small town sheriff. His wife had escaped, and his biggest fear, based upon the detached manner in which she'd treated him, of late, was that she'd be coming for him next. He didn't know why, and he didn't know when, but he had a deep sense of foreboding telling him that his wife wasn't going to just leave him alone. She was coming for him, he felt sure of it.

"That's an awfully low price for a home like yours, Mr. Eckels," the perky brunette realtor told him gravely. "I'm sure we can get a better price. The property is in good shape, and..." she began.

"Sell it at that price," Tim's voice held no expression. "I'll contact you with information as to where to send the proceeds."

"Oh, you're moving right away?" The realtor's brows rose.

"I'll be traveling."

"I see," she nodded, not seeing at all, but growing more uncomfortable by the minute, just being in the same room with the husband of a vicious serial killer.

She'd seen Susannah's story on the news, and was just desperate enough for a new listing that she'd agreed to meet him at the unassuming little cottage next to the mortuary.

"I'll appreciate your...discretion in dealing with this matter," Tim looked her in the eye momentarily, then glanced away.

He'd never been one to maintain eye contact. People disturbed him, generally. His job as a mortician had given him a supreme appreciation of the permanently somnolent human form, but he'd never quite managed to acquire much enthusiasm for those who were still animated.

Tim was selling the house and its contents, that is, any of the articles that had been left behind after the evidence techs had gone, for much less than it was worth. He wanted to sever all ties with this community, and with Susannah. His only instinct was to run. He didn't know where he'd go, or what he'd do once he got there, but staying in the now-too-small town wasn't an option. His goal was to maintain a low profile, in hopes that Susannah would never find him. He didn't know whether she'd seek comfort from him, or kill him, but didn't want to take the chance, not feeling at all comfortable with either option. The terrifying reality, which crossed Tim's mind, was that she never really seemed to need much comfort.

Pulling out of his driveway for the last time, Tim glanced in his rearview mirror, and saw the mortuary where he'd begun his career. He'd been the best...and only, undertaker in town, and had received glowing praise for his artistry in preparing the dead and maintaining a dignified sanctuary in which to say goodbye to the deceased. Loved ones had shaken his hand, tears in their eyes, and thanked him for his work. He'd been respected, if not admired, and now he had to walk away. From the work that he loved, a town where he'd almost been accepted, and the only woman he'd ever...been with. Love was too strong a word for what they'd had. They'd coexisted in a manner which had been acceptable to both of them.

He had no map. He had no destination in mind. Everything he'd known was gone. Tim headed south, to a new life. The shadow of the killer he'd married loomed large, but he was drawn to find the sunlight.

CHAPTER THREE

The cloying scent of the artificial Cherry Blossom soap spray that she'd used for an impromptu shower at a self-serve car wash wasn't exactly something that Susannah relished, but when an opportunity to get clean and look somewhat normal had surfaced, she'd jumped on it. Limping into the Quad Cities, where Iowa met Illinois, feet covered with blisters, her clothing still vaguely damp, and her ribs beginning to protrude, she wanted nothing more than a hot meal and a decent bed, but she knew that she'd probably have to kill to get them. It was time to feed that need anyway, so she'd be smart about it and use the experience to begin to form her new reality.

She'd had plenty of time to concoct a plan for staying alive and off of the police radar while she jogged through farm country. A city the size of

Bettendorf, one of the Quad Cities, was just big enough that she should be able to slip in, choose a victim, kill her and steal her identity, then continue on to the Windy City. Susannah knew just the type of woman that she was looking for, and just where to find her. Her introverted years of fading into the background and observing people, were about to come in quite handy.

Rolling a homeless man who snored in a drunken slumber under a bridge had been all too easy. He'd barely stirred, and when he'd seen the crazed eyes of the woman who was digging through his stiff, urine-stained pants pockets, he'd passed out again immediately. Apparently, he wasn't a terribly successful panhandler, he only had three dollars and some change on him, but that would suit Susannah's purposes well enough. She didn't even consider killing the pathetic soul. Word traveled fast in homeless communities, and she didn't want to spook anyone with a murder. The homeless provided easy resources for her - getting supplies from them was like taking candy from a baby - and it might take a while to put her plan to change her identity into action, so she'd refrain from killing any of them, at least until her immediate mission was accomplished, and she could move on to the next phase of her plan.

Standing in line at a bustling coffee shop near the mall, Susannah spotted her target. There was a young woman with close-cropped auburn hair, who wore a tired outfit that looked as though it had been purchased in the seventies. It screamed vintage thrift shop. The fact that she was staring intently at a small tablet in front of her, told Susannah some of what she wanted to know. The target had shabby, artsy clothes and didn't have a laptop, which meant that she probably didn't have much money. Her disappearance wouldn't be splashed across every news channel in the region. In fact, it might not merit even the slightest mention. She sat alone, which hopefully meant that she didn't have too many close ties, and she was in a coffee shop in the middle of the day, signaling that she either didn't have a job, or had one that was non-traditional. She clearly fancied herself to be one of those creative types, who could disappear at any moment without raising a single eyebrow. Perfect.

Susannah purchased a black coffee because it was cheap, despite her disdain for the noxious liquid, and grimaced when she smelled the aroma of burnt beans that had been in the roaster just a shade too long. Having been classically trained as a chef had given her a good nose for quality, and a supreme loathing for mediocrity when it came to food and drink. This place was one she would have never walked into if it hadn't been such an obvious haven for artistic waifs.

"Hi! Can I sit here?" she asked the target brightly, channeling the personality of a cheerleader that she remembered from high school.

The young woman looked up, startled, and blinked at Susannah stupidly for a moment, then looked around the crowded coffee shop before nodding.

"Uh, yeah, sure," was the less than enthusiastic reply.

She reached over and pulled a worn olive-drab backpack from the only other chair at the small, faux wood-grained table.

"Thanks. I've been at the mall all day and I really just wanted a change of scenery," Susannah hoped that her opener would engage the woman in conversation.

"Oh, yeah, I bet. I don't really shop at malls," the target replied, staring down at her tablet.

"Work?" Susannah asked, nodding her head at the tablet.

"Nah, I'm just killing time. I work from home," she shrugged.

"That must be tough if you have roommates," the killer probed, sipping her bilious brew.

"Oh, I don't. I'm not much of a people person," the target attempted a smile, but it looked more like she was experiencing a particularly uncomfortable gas bubble.

Bingo.

"Me neither. What do you do?" Susannah persisted, working hard to feign interest.

"I'm a writer. Well, I'm trying to be anyway. I do freelance work."

The killer in the coffee shop could hardly contain her glee – a friendless, groundless millennial – she couldn't have picked a more perfect target.

"Wow, that's fascinating. What do you write?"

Susannah remembered that the secret to having a normal conversation, from what she'd read on the subject, was to appear interested in the other person and to ask questions about them. She couldn't care less about the young woman's freelancing career, but she nodded and made positive noises, as the target gave her a rather brief explanation. The killer pretended to be fascinated, all the while waiting for an opening to try to move closer to her goal. A question from the unmotivated young woman hung in the air between them, while Susannah made murderous plans, and she only realized it when the target stared at her expectantly, waiting for an answer.

"I'm sorry, what?" the preoccupied killer asked, pasting on a plastic smile.

"I said, what do you do?" the target repeated, a little more loudly.

"Oh, well. I'm still trying to figure that out," Susannah shrugged. "I went to culinary school, but I just didn't want to work in my dad's restaurant," she lied, making up the story as she went along. "They expected me to live and think like they do, and I just had to get out, you know? I like to do sculpture, and I'm really trying to figure out how to maybe make a living doing that."

The target nodded, hooked.

"So, here I am in the Quad Cities, just an over-educated girl with no job, no place to go, and hardly any money left. All of my art supplies are at home, and I'm feeling really...creative right now. It's frustrating. Do you ever feel like that?" Susannah sighed dramatically, hoping that she wasn't being too over the top.

"Story of my life," the target grimaced. "I

wanted to go to art school because I like to paint and I think I do an okay job of it, but the parental units wouldn't shell out money for it. That wasn't "real" education," she made air quotes with her fingers.

"Typical," Susannah shook her head, feigning disgust.

The young woman stared at Susannah across the table, with an expression which seemed like commiseration, but then she frowned, as if suddenly having realized something. "If you don't have any money, what were you doing at the mall?"

"It was a place to sit. They have clean bathrooms, and sometimes people drop money," Susannah shrugged, kicking herself for telling such an obvious lie earlier. "I'm not proud of it, but a girl's gotta survive, you know?"

"I hear ya," the young woman agreed.

"So, are you working on any paintings right now?" Susannah was inspired, an idea brewing.

The target shifted in her seat, looking a bit embarrassed.

"Yeah. So...I've been dealing with some depression and stuff lately, and I'm working on this piece called "Blue." It's kind of a self-portrait, that's done all in shades of blue, with some black and grey for shadowing. There are lots of shadows," she added, her gaze dropping to the tabletop.

"I express my feelings through my art too, and there's plenty of darkness, so I get it," Susannah nodded, thinking how truthful her statement really was.

The young woman looked up, surprised. "Yeah?" she asked.

"Yeah, definitely. I mean, when I can't handle things sometimes...I just have to create, you know?" the killer began laying the groundwork for her plan.

"Exactly. I have one called "Fuck Society" that's really cool," the target volunteered with a cynical smile.

"Sounds like we have a lot in common," Susannah smiled. "I'd love to see your work some-time, if you feel like sharing it, that is. I totally understand if it's too personal. I don't let hardly anyone see my pieces."

"I usually don't share my stuff. It's not like I have people beating down the door to see it," the young woman said sourly. "But, you sound like you might actually be able to appreciate it."

"One artist to another," Susannah shrugged, not wanting to seem too eager.

"Well, I'm not doing anything tonight, if you

want to stop by," the target offered, blushing a bit. Susannah totally related to her social awkwardness, feeling keenly uncomfortable herself.

"I have nothing going on, so yeah, that'd be cool."

"I'm not good company or anything. You can probably tell that."

"Me neither," Susannah smiled faintly. "But it's all about the art, right?"

"Right," the target seemed relieved.

She scrawled her name and address on a scrap of paper and handed it to the killer, not realizing that she had just signed her death warrant.

"See you tonight," Susannah waved the paper, as the target stuffed her tablet into her backpack, preparing to leave.

"Don't expect much," the depressed woman warned, a strange look flitting across her features.

"I'm open-minded," Susannah assured her. Open-minded indeed.

The place was a dump. The target, whose name was Angelica, lived in an apartment atop a liquor store, which was accessed by a back door that opened into an alley redolent with the smell of garbage and exhaust.

"It's small, and it's shitty, but it's all I've got," Angelica announced when she opened the door, letting Susannah into a home that was as dark and messy as its inhabitant.

"Better than where I came from," Susannah lied, remembering the cozy cottage that she'd shared with her soft-spoken husband, Tim. Their furnishings had been simple, but the house had been immaculate, a product of a bit of OCD in both of them. Their relationship hadn't been dynamic, but it had been easy, giving both of them a great deal of personal time.

"Do you have a separate room for your art studio?" Susannah asked, taking stock of the untidy apartment.

"No, this place is tiny. I paint in one end of my bedroom. You can sit on the couch if you want and I'll bring the paintings out to show you. Sometimes the springs stick up through the cushions, and it kinda smells like my grandma, but it's pretty comfortable," Angelica called out, retreating to her bedroom.

"Gotcha. Do you mind if I use your bathroom?"

Susannah asked, wanting to further explore the layout.

"Go for it. Just turn the light out when you're done, I try to minimize my impact on the environment," the would-be writer instructed.

Angelica didn't like people much, but apparently, she cared about the planet. Susannah rolled her eyes. People who were walking stereotypes annoyed her to no end.

"Great," she replied, trying her best to sound pleasant.

She headed down the hall to the bathroom and shuddered at what she saw when she flipped on the light. No wonder Angelica wanted to keep this room in the dark. The countertop around the small sink was cluttered with organic makeup, essential oils, boxes of feminine products, trash and clothing, and the shower had black shadows of mold growing in the corners and up the walls. Susannah was profoundly glad that she had her shoes on, just so she didn't have to make contact with the floor of the dusty, sticky, hair-strewn bathroom. The shower curtain would provide good coverage against spilled blood eventually, and there were manicure scissors on the back of the toilet, just for fun. She made a mental note.

"Well, here they are," Angelica waved vaguely at two paintings which were leaning against a dingy wall, side by side, in what passed for her living room.

Susannah rose from her seat on the musty couch, folded her arms and nodded, acting as though she was studying the grossly amateur offerings before her.

"This is beyond what I had expected," she remarked.

That much was true. She'd actually been hoping that Angelica would've had at least some talent.

"Thanks," there was the insecure embarrassment again, evidenced by her dropped gaze.

The two of them stood in silence for a while, Susannah pretending to gaze at the paintings while she plotted her next move, Angelica staring at Susannah pensively.

"It's weird..." Angelica commented, frowning.

Susannah's stomach turned over when she heard those words and saw the target studying her closely.

"I feel like I know you from somewhere."

Susannah noticed the slow and steady pulse beating lightly in Angelica's neck, and a shiver of longing ran through her. She smiled.

"Look in the mirror," Susannah murmured, her eyes returning to the painting. "We could be sisters."

Which was more than she had dared to hope for. It had been a brilliant streak of luck that she had found someone who looked very much like her. It would make using the victim's driver's license and bank card much easier. Susannah hoped against hope that she didn't look familiar to Angelica because of a wanted poster or something. There was a process that she wanted to follow, and panic on the part of her target could turn her neat little plan upside down.

"Yeah, maybe that's it. So, which one do you like best?" Angelica's attention returned to the paintings, much to Susannah's relief.

"Apples and oranges," the killer replied. "You really can't compare the two."

"You DO get it," Angelica breathed a sigh of relief, a ghost of a smile playing about her lips.

"Oh, I get it all right," Susannah turned to her with murder in her eyes.

The lust to kill rose up in her like a smothering red mist, consuming her. Every nerve in her body tingled with anticipation.

CHAPTER FOUR

It wasn't so much that Tim was a patient man, it was more that he saved his angst for things that really mattered. Which was why it baffled him that the traffic in Indianapolis infuriated him. There was no drumming of his fingers on the steering wheel, he was too fatigued for even that physical expression of his impatience. No, the sign that gave away his growing frustration was the occasional sigh and clenching of his jaw. He'd driven through the night, and thus forgave himself for having a typically human reaction to his present circumstances. He was tired. And cranky. And he hadn't had any of his wife's amazing home cooking for quite some time. No, he didn't miss her, or even her cooking, specifically, he was just tired of fast food and gas station snacks.

A yellow and black sign advertising waffles caught his attention, and as much as he hated eating in public – it made him feel vulnerable – he knew that he needed sustenance, and sooner rather than later. Assuming that the traffic would have time to ebb a bit as he ate, he pulled off the interstate and into the parking lot. The restaurant was in a part of town that seemed altogether unsavory, and the mild-mannered mortician would stick out like a sore thumb, but he didn't care. He needed food.

The hostess seated him in a vinyl-covered booth which faced the windows. Hung in a corner opposite him was an ancient television, tuned to a local station, which blared a newscast. He ordered his breakfast, along with a cup of coffee and a glass of juice, idly watching the screen. Its bleak offerings were actually far more appealing than the blighted scene outside the window. Tim's heart leapt into his throat as Susannah's picture flashed onto the screen. She was a fugitive now, and the hunt had grown into a nationwide one. He'd hoped that local law enforcement would have apprehended her, but he knew, deep down inside, that she was much too diabolically clever to be taken in that easily.

There were rewards offered for information as to her whereabouts, and a tip line had been established. The relief at not seeing his own picture beside hers was profound. He'd wondered when he left town so abruptly whether or not the clueless sheriff would put out a warrant for his arrest, but so far, it would seem that he was in the clear. He'd done nothing wrong, but he knew that often times, as the wheels of justice ground up citizens and spat them out, trivial details like innocence didn't matter.

The server set down his plate and he noticed that one of the yolks of his eggs had broken and was oozing thickly into the edge of a heap of greasy hash browns. The sight made him sad somehow. The disorder of it all representing the mess that his life had become.

"Can I get ya anything else, hon?" the tired-looking young woman asked, snapping her gum like punctuation.

Tim hated it when strangers used pet names. They didn't know him. He wasn't her 'hon.' He no longer had a hon, and this server shouldn't presume that he'd be her 'hon.' Realizing how cranky this thought was, Tim merely asked for more white toast and dropped his gaze back to his plate. He'd consumed both pieces of bacon, the unbroken egg, two slices of toast, and half of the hash browns, when a police car pulled into the parking lot.

Tim used his peripheral vision, no easy task, considering the thickness of his horn-rimmed glasses, to watch the approach of the cruiser. He hoped that it would merely drive through the parking lot, on its way to somewhere else. Anywhere else. It didn't. His heart hammered in his chest and he couldn't eat another bite. He had serious doubts about whether he'd actually be able to swallow the bite he was currently chewing, which had somehow turned to sawdust in his throat.

Raising a hand, he waved the server over and asked for his check. He must have been acting strangely, because she tilted her head and stared at him quizzically.

"You want me to box that up for you, hon?" she asked, glancing down at his plate.

Tim's eyes darted to the door, where two policemen entered, then back again.

"Uh, no. Thank you. I'm traveling," he explained, pulling out a twenty and handing it to her.

"Okay, I'll go get your change," she promised, starting to walk away.

"Keep the change," Tim instructed, brushing by her and heading for the men's restroom.

"You sure?" she called after him, eyes wide.

He didn't turn around. The hostess was leading

the policemen to a table, and Tim stepped around them, pretending to look at his watch. When he got into the restroom, the pale face staring back at him looked tired, worn and terrified.

"I have to relax," he whispered to his reflection, noting the crinkles at the corner of his eyes and the tension making a pale rictus of his mouth. "I look suspicious. I didn't do anything. I can do this," he took a deep breath.

Having splashed icy tap water on his face, he waved his hand under the automatic paper towel dispenser. As it cranked out a swath of paper towel, with a mechanical whine, the door to the restroom opened, and one of the police officers entered. Tim's blood pressure rose so rapidly, and with such force, that it felt like his head might explode. The cop stepped toward him.

"You alright, buddy?" he asked, his eyes assessing the pale man.

"I'm good. Too many waffles, I guess," Tim made a sick attempt at a smile.

The cop stared at him. A trickle of sweat ran cold down the back of Tim's neck and trailed down his spine. He felt it soak into the waistband of his trousers and was disgusted by it.

"Maybe I should get the pancakes then, huh?"

the sharp-eyed cop smiled, finally. "Take care now," he said, stepping into a stall.

"You too," Tim made a herculean effort to sound normal.

A wave of nausea struck, and he braced himself on the sink, clenching his teeth to keep his breakfast down. Taking a deep breath, he headed for the door. Still holding his paper towel so that he didn't have to touch the handle, he opened it, and made a beeline for the exit. Walking at a normal pace was a challenge, when all he wanted to do was bolt from the establishment, and he had to remind himself to unclench his fists, holding his hands stiffly at his sides.

He felt the eyes of the police boring into his back as he slid into the driver's seat, and made certain that he fastened his seat belt and pulled out of the parking lot slowly. Easing back onto the highway, he was relieved to see that traffic was flowing much better now, and he accelerated steadily, putting as much space as possible between himself and the waffle restaurant.

CHAPTER FIVE

"I'll just tell you right now, I really hate this," Susannah spoke softly to her victim in the early hours before dawn.

While she generally despised interaction, it had been so long since she'd been able to enjoy a murder that she had taken her time preparing Angelica, engaging in conversation with her long into the night to figure out what she was about. She needed to find a legitimate reason to kill her, and to determine which methods the unwitting victim would find most horrifying. She wanted to enjoy this one, so it had to be profound. She quivered, just thinking of it.

Susannah, whenever possible, made a point to choose her victims carefully. She chose men, mostly, because she despised bullies who manipulated those weaker than themselves, and she looked specifically for identifying traits like arrogance and conceit. While Angelica, on the surface, had none of the obvious characteristics, Susannah had carefully uncovered a tragic flaw. The young woman was the epitome of a victim. She took responsibility for nothing, including her own lot in life and lack of achievement, blaming everyone from her teachers to her parents to society at large. While this wasn't normally a qualifying factor in Susannah's world, the harsh reality was that she needed to steal Angelica's identity, which would be problematic if she let her live, so the weak rationalization would just have to do.

While her target had slipped away for a moment to use the bathroom, blissfully unaware, Susannah had popped into the kitchen, donning yellow latex gloves, which had clearly never been used. Glancing down at the vinyl floor, which was peeling around the edges, she'd remembered that the shower curtain that she needed to prep her murder scene was currently hanging in the bathroom with the victim. She'd have to subdue and secure Angelica before she could proceed with setting the stage, harvesting her souvenirs, and eventually bringing the young woman's short, self-destructive life to a close.

Angelica yawned loudly as she came down the hall toward the kitchen. "Hey, Suze, I hate to bring this party to an end, but," her sentence was abruptly cut off as she entered the kitchen, entirely unaware that a serial killer awaited her, hidden by the refrigerator.

Choosing the easiest method of silencing someone, particularly a spindly female, Susannah popped out from behind the fridge and punched Angelica in the face as hard as she could. There was a satisfying crunch as her knuckles made contact with her victim's nose and mouth, but she really wished that she could have chosen a cleaner, more sophisticated method of subduing the young woman. Brute force was never her first choice. Knives were so much more elegant.

Angelica slumped to the floor like a sack of potatoes and Susannah left her there, strolling to the bathroom to collect the moldy shower curtain. When she returned to the kitchen, the killer had plenty of time to spread out the shower curtain and rifle through the drawers to find a suitable murder weapon, along with a roll of duct tape. Rejecting knife after pitiful pitted and scarred knife, she finally settled on a large butcher knife.

"It'll have to do," she shook her head, appalled at the condition of her chosen instrument of death.

A pristinely sharpened utensil was a thing of beauty, and this abomination wasn't even close to pristine, but it would get the job done.

"This will hurt worse," she mused, holding the blade up to the light. "She should've taken better care of her things."

Susannah sat on Angelica's abdomen, happy that her prey had regained consciousness, her knees pinning the terrified young woman's arms to her sides. Angelica's breath sounded like a steam engine as it puffed in and out through her mangled nose, because her mouth had been securely duct taped, broken teeth and all. Susannah smiled when she thought of the pain that would be involved in pulling the duct tape from the split lip below it. She'd have bruised knuckles for a few days due to the force of impact, but it had been totally worth it, just to have subdued her victim so efficiently. Angelica made a thin moaning sound and Susannah reached down to pinch her nostrils shut.

"Now, don't do that," Susannah cautioned, as Angelica turned an alarming shade of red due to panic, pain, and a lack of oxygen. "I can't have you making noises," she chided. "Are you going to be quiet?"

Angelica nodded furiously, gasping and whistling through her bleeding nose when Susannah released it. Her chest heaved with effort. A bubble of blood, mixed with snot, bloomed under one swollen nostril.

"That's disgusting," Susannah grimaced, poking at the bubble with the tip of the butcher knife, causing Angelica to flinch, her eyes going wide.

"Oh, stop being so dramatic," she tapped Angelica on the tip of the nose with the knife. "You'll know when I'm going to hurt you. I'll warn you. Now, as I was saying…I hate to do this, because you really seemed kind of nice, if a bit stupid, inviting a total stranger in, even though you don't really like people, but…I have to do this. It's all part of a bigger plan. You're just a cog in the machine at this point, which I know must upset you, but it's all for the best. Your life wasn't going anywhere anyway, and this filthy house would've killed you eventually," Susannah said in a matter-of-fact tone.

Angelica's eyes filled with tears.

"Don't make a sound," Susannah reminded her, wiggling the knife above her eyes, as her breath shuddered in and out in horror. An idea struck the killer suddenly. "Wait! Do you have tattoos? I bet you do, don't you?" she brightened at the thought.

Tattoos made very pretty souvenirs.

"Let's see," she mused. "If I were young and pretending to be wild, where would my tattoos be...?"

She secured Angelica's hands with duct tape, then flipped her over onto her stomach, lifting up the hem of her cotton t-shirt.

"Yep, tramp stamp. How did I know?" she shook her head. "I like dolphins, I'll take it. I bet you have another one on your bikini line, don't you?" she asked, not expecting an answer from the trussed up young woman.

She turned her back over, yanking down the front of her sleep shorts, and was disappointed that there were no tattoos under the pale pink panties on Angelica's slim hips.

"Oh yeah, one more spot," she commented, moving down to where the young woman's feet were bound together at the ankles. "I didn't see one on your ankles, but I bet...yup, there it is. A butterfly. That'll be a great way to start my new collection," Susannah said, after peeling back a blue fuzzy ankle sock and finding the tattoo on the top of Angelica's foot.

"I would've preferred more yellow, but an orange butterfly will be nice too. The color will darken a bit once it cures," she murmured, grasping Angelica under the arms and dragging her onto the shower curtain, where the real fun would begin, while the young woman struggled feebly.

The millennial's artistic inclinations had obviously precluded her from spending any quality time in the gym, and she was no match for Susannah's determined strength. Once the killer had maneuvered her onto the plastic, she perched atop her again, looking down into the depths of her eyes. When Angelica's eyes widened and her breathing became intense again, Susannah shushed her, tapping on her forehead.

"Quiet now. I usually take my souvenirs first, then kill, but you were rather nice to me, despite your hatred of humanity, so I'll kill you now, then take your pretty tattoos," she smiled, anticipating the dramatic manifestation of terror that typically accompanied such statements.

Angelica's pitiful moans were eerie as they rattled through her inflamed sinuses, causing the blood to burble up and trail down her cheeks.

"Don't make me change my mind, Angelica," Susannah held the tip of her knife to the ultra-sensitive space between her victim's eyes, piercing just the tiniest bit.

The pain seemed to bring sharp focus to the struggling victim. She stilled, and though her throat worked, producing awful, guttural sounds, she stopped the high-pitched whining. A thin line of blood trickled into her eye, and she blinked rapidly. Her breathing slowed, and her body completely went slack as she gave in to her fate.

"Wow, that's amazing," Susannah observed, lifting the knife. "No one ever just gives up like that. You didn't really like your life, did you? Death isn't the worst possible thing that could happen to you, am I right?" she asked. "Blink twice if you agree."

Blink. Blink. No hesitation. A dying girl's last sad statement.

"I respect that. You're no coward, Angelica. I'm going to make this one quick."

Susannah expertly sliced open her carotid with a flick of the wrist, and held a black plastic garbage sack to the wound to catch the blood. Angelica's body shuddered a couple of times, but she passed out mercifully quickly. Duct-taping the bag around the wound, and elevating her feet to make her bleed out more quickly, Susannah went to work excising the butterfly tattoo. She knew she'd have to wait to have access to the dolphins which frolicked at Angelica's belt line, but there were things to be done, and she had the luxury of being able to take her time.

CHAPTER SIX

Tim had driven for twelve hours after leaving the waffle restaurant in Indianapolis, stopping only a handful of times to put fuel in the car, relieve himself and purchase tidbits of the grease-dipped, batter-encrusted types of food that are sold at gas stations and convenience marts. He was exhausted, and as he pulled into a rest area, just north of the Florida state line, he knew that sleeping was no longer merely a good idea, but a necessity. He could, quite literally, not keep his eyes open.

Finding a parking spot far away from the restrooms and vending machines, he tilted his seat back and gave in to the exhaustion that had been trying to lure him into slumber for about the past one hundred miles or so. Mouth open, he snored with abandon, blissfully unaware of the world outside of his vehicle. That is, until an insistent tapping startled him awake.

How long he'd been asleep, Tim had no idea. He sat bolt upright, his neck stiff, his heart pounding, and saw that the sun had set. Quite a while ago, by the looks of it. The harsh beam of a flashlight shone in his face and he winced, turning away from it.

"Georgia State Patrol, sir. I'm going to need you to step out of the car," a voice ordered, through the closed window.

A surge of adrenaline shot through Tim. He couldn't see with the light shining in his face, so he didn't even know whether running to escape would be possible. The police had tracked him down. They couldn't find Susannah, so they wanted to punish him in her stead. His sleep-clouded mind went into panic mode, and he sat behind the steering wheel, blinking, not knowing what to do.

"Sir, I need you to step out of the car," the pot-bellied patrolman, with the molasses-thick southern drawl, tapped on the window again, with his nightstick, by the sound of it.

In his current circumstance, there was no escape. He hadn't done anything wrong, other than choose a serial killer as his mate, so perhaps they'd go easy on him. Resigned to whatever possible fate might await him, he slowly reached for the door handle, and opened the door. Not being a great conversationalist in general, and not knowing what to say to a police officer, specifically, he got out and kept quiet, trying his best to see around the green splotches in his eyes, caused by the flashlight.

"I'm going to need your driver's license, proof of insurance, and registration," the cop said, training the beam of his flashlight on the interior of the car.

"I have my license in my wallet, but the others are in the glove compartment," Tim replied, wondering why the cop hadn't asked for those items before he got out of the car.

"Go ahead and get them for me, please," the patrolman directed.

Tim knelt on the driver's seat and reached across to open the glove compartment. He kept a black vinyl folder in there, which contained the requested documents. The officer kept the flashlight beam steady so that Tim could see to fish the documents out. He stood and handed them over.

"You're a long way from home," the officer commented, checking the address on both documents.

"Yep," Tim replied, having heard that it was better to keep statements to the police brief.

"Where ya headed?" the cop asked, looking back and forth between Tim and the papers.

"South," Tim looked curiously at the cop.

Clearly, he was headed south...it was even on the highway sign. The cop stared at him for a moment, looking as though he was trying to determine whether Tim was joking or not.

"Business or pleasure?" he asked, his tone perceptibly cooler.

"Both."

"Got any weapons on you or in the vehicle?"

"No, sir."

Tim's stomach rolled miserably. If the cop chose to run his license through the system, he might connect him to Susannah, which might mean getting hauled in for questioning. He just wanted to get away from the horrible memories of tragedy. What his wife had done was not his fault, yet here he stood, sweating and nauseated.

"Drugs?"

"Definitely not."

Tim swallowed, hearing an audible click as the dryness of his throat caused it to constrict.

"Why were you sleeping here in the rest area? Camping overnight isn't allowed," the cop handed Tim his license and paperwork.

Tim nearly fainted with relief.

"Oh, I wasn't going to sleep here overnight. I stopped this morning, just for a few hours. I drive during the night because there's less traffic on the road."

"Go ahead and get back into your vehicle and head on down the road then. I'm gonna come back by here a couple of times tonight, and if I find you here, I'm going to ticket you for loitering. Understood?"

The cop hitched up his gun belt.

"Yes, sir."

"Drive safe out there."

"You too," Tim replied, hurriedly ducking into his car.

He stepped a bit too hard on the gas, backing out of his parking space, and winced, hoping he wasn't calling undue attention to himself. He drove very carefully, and the police car pulled out behind him, trailing him to the on-ramp for the highway, and following closely once he'd merged into the fast-flowing traffic. Tim had an urgent need for the bathroom, but he would try to make it as far as he could before finding a gas station where he could stop. By the time he found an appropriate exit, the cop had moved on, and Tim practically sprinted into the mini-mart.

He'd never hated another human being in his life, though he had at least a mild disdain for most of them. As he bellied up to the urinal however, his kidneys aching, Susannah's name was on his lips, and his mutterings were less than kind.

CHAPTER SEVEN

Her plan had come together so quickly and easily that Susannah wondered what she had done to deserve such dumb luck. After she finished draining the blood from Angelica, disposing of it in the filthy shower, she loaded up the worn and tired backpack with clothing, her souvenirs, which were carefully packaged in foil and tucked in plastic baggies, and other miscellaneous supplies, then drove the dead woman's car to a spot just outside her door in the alley. She'd set the tattoos in a low oven for a few hours while she prepared to go, so by the time she packed them, they were well on their way to being dried out and ready to use as art. Having patched up the missing tattoo wounds with duct tape so that they didn't seep even a little bit, she slung one of Angelica's lifeless arms around her neck, and hoisted her onto her hip, making it appear as though the two were walking arm in arm.

Affecting a drunken slur, Susannah staggered out the back door with Angelica in the hours just before dawn.

"So, I told that jerk that I wasn't gonna go with him. It's ladies night and you and me are gonna live it up," she told the dead woman in her arms, "helping" her into the backseat.

In Angelica's dingy, apathetic neighborhood, she was fairly certain that there would be no crusading neighbors coming out to lecture her on the ills of buzzed driving. She was correct. Not a soul was about.

She sat the corpse upright, buckled her into the seat, and headed for an abandoned grain elevator that she'd scoped out on her way into town. It was in a remote location which suited her purpose perfectly. She'd only found it because she'd been following the railroad tracks which eventually led into town, but looking at the map had shown her the closest farm road where she could park and drag or carry Angelica the rest of the way. The locks on the doors were broken, weeds and dust had claimed the interior, and not a soul had set foot in the shabby structure for a very long time.

"I'm going to get your clothes dirty, Angelica," Susannah looked ruefully down at the jeans and t-shirt that she had borrowed from the dead girl's closet, comforted by the fact that she had plenty of replacements in her bag.

Having disposed of the body, as well as the clothing that she'd been wearing while handling the body, Susannah drove back to town, a lock of Angelica's hair in her pocket. She took hair as a souvenir generally, but this time she had a specific purpose for doing so. Standing in front of an array of dyes in the grocery store, she pulled the hairs out and compared them to the color swatches on the top of the boxes until she found the closest match.

Standing in front of the hazy bathroom mirror in Angelica's hovel, Susannah snipped at her long, dirty blonde tresses, trying to approximate the length of the dead woman's hair. Once she was satisfied with the cut, she slipped on the plastic gloves that came with the hair dye and applied the thick, gloppy mixture to her newly shorn locks, which immediately took on a mahogany sheen. It looked like it was going to be darker than Angelica's had been, but as long as it was in the same color family, she figured that it would be close enough. After showering without the missing curtain, and not caring that the spray went all over the disgusting floor, she combed her newly-colorful hair, arranging it in the same spiky, tousled way that Angelica had. Slipping into another clean set of the dead woman's jeans and a t-shirt, she looked in the mirror.

"Well hello, Angelica," she murmured, impressed with the results.

Admiring her skill, and tying the bag of her shorn locks securely shut, to be disposed of later, Susannah turned her attention to Angelica's tablet, which she planned to take with her when she left the Quad Cities. With a few taps on the smudged screen, she had access to all of the dead woman's social media accounts, banking information, which was rather dismal, and her freelance work accounts.

"First things first," she muttered, reading the inane posts on Angelica's social media sites.

It took her a moment to figure out how to post, but once she did, having read enough of the millennial's posts to figure out her phrasing and slang habits, she posted a message for the few friends that the wannabe writer had.

Hey everybody. I'm going off grid for a while, if anyone cares. There's gotta be more to life than paying bills, so I'm not gonna. Sorry credit card company, you'll just have to survive without my interest charges. I may come back on here, I may not, but either way, I'll be trying to live the dream...my way. Peace.

Rifling through the dead woman's olive-drab backpack, shortly after Angelica's demise, Susannah had discovered a debit card, a credit card, a driver's license, social security card, and a punch card for the coffee shop where they'd met. A quick check on the tablet showed that Angelica had exactly $78 in her bank account, and a balance of $436.29 on her credit card, with just over $100 in available credit. It wasn't much, but it would at least get her out of town. She had a new identity, clothes and a car, and tomorrow at first light, she'd be on her way.

"Chicago," Susannah murmured to herself as she perused the gas station map. "It's not that far, and I'll be able to be anonymous."

Buckling her seat belt, she headed east, toward her new life.

While Susannah loved the freedom and anonymity of the city, she hated the noise and the smell of that much humanity gathered in one spot. On the plus side, though, the noise would mask the screams of the dying, and the smell would cover the scent of death. Perfect.

She ditched the car in a dark, seedy-looking spot under the L train, and set about finding her way around the city. Angelica's meager funds wouldn't last very long, but she hoped to find her own resources in short order. She carried a few food items that she'd scavenged from Angelica's filthy kitchen, but found herself craving a hot meal. With the paltry amount of cash that she'd pilfered from her victim's purse and bedroom, she could at least afford a hearty meal at a diner. She'd have to be careful about her eating habits, though, because Angelica's license said that she weighed a hundred and twenty pounds. Susannah had lost a significant amount of weight since escaping the small-town jail, but wasn't quite that small yet. She was also three inches taller than her victim, so she hoped that she never had occasion to use the identification that she'd stolen.

Walking for miles, keeping to back streets and alleys, Susannah found herself in a part of the city which, while not run-down and dangerous, certainly didn't have the glitz and glamour of the Gold Coast, or the overcrowding issues of the favorite spots among the tourists. She was in an ordinary neighborhood which seemed to lean bohemian. It was an ideal area for her to fade into the background and take stock of her options. With any luck, she'd find someone worth killing. Angelica's death had rekindled her need for blood and power, and the thrill of it had ignited another need within her that only her Timmy could fill. She yearned for him, physically, having made a habit of coming home from a kill and demanding his sexual attention. Not being able to satisfy either of her primal appetites would make for a very dangerous Susannah.

Passing by a tired-looking row of brownstones, she noticed a crudely painted sign which said, "Co-op Kitchen." There was an obviously hand-drawn arrow on the sign, pointing toward the alley between the somewhat shabby homes.

"The food probably sucks, but there may be some naïve types there, just begging to be taken advantage of," she mused, heading down the alley, where the wind caused various pieces of trash to skitter along like filthy, human-generated leaves.

A few hundred feet down the alley was a purple

door with the letters "CK" painted on it in yellow.

"Well, I'm guessing this isn't Calvin Klein's house," Susannah rolled her eyes, and tried the door handle.

Locked. Her stomach growling, she gritted her teeth and turned back toward the way that she'd come.

"Hey, sorry about that," a voice called out to her from the now-open purple door. "We forgot to unlock the door when we opened back up this afternoon," a smiling young man with hair to his waist explained. "Want some food?"

"Yeah," Susannah attempted a smile and trudged toward the Co-op Kitchen, hoping against hope that it wasn't a vegan establishment.

These kinds of co-ops were often run by tree-hugging hippies who pampered animals rather than eating them, and she needed real food.

"Hi, I'm Devin. Ever been here before?" the young man, who smelled vaguely of patchouli, asked, opening the door wider so that she could pass.

"Hi. Uh, no. I'm new in town," Susannah entered the dark interior, momentarily unable to see.

"Oh, cool. Well, welcome to Co-op Kitchen. We believe in sharing resources, so if you'd like to donate money for your meal, that'll work, but if you'd rather do dishes or help us cook or whatever, you can do that too," he shrugged, still smiling.

"I'm pretty good in the kitchen," Susannah volunteered, her eyes adjusting to the light.

This would be like taking candy from a baby. The Co-op still looked like the shabby house that it once was, inside. Devin led her through a small living room, and they wound their way between a handful of tables set up in the dining room. There was a tantalizing fragrance in the air, coming from the direction of what was obviously the kitchen.

"Sweet," Devin nodded. "Come with me. What's your name?" he asked, leading her into a kitchen that hadn't been updated since the seventies.

"Uh...Angelica," she had to think for a second, and hoped that he hadn't noticed her hesitation, or had at least mistaken it for shyness.

"Great name," he replied, the look on his face reminding her of an adoring puppy.

She happened to glance down and notice that he was barefoot. The thought of that in a kitchen made her shudder.

"This is Shiloh, she's making the dinner stuff for tonight, so she'll hook you up with some tasks," Devin pointed at a very pregnant dark-haired woman who was chopping vegetables at a huge butcher block island. "Shiloh, this is Angelica. She wants some food and says that she's good in the kitchen."

"Hi, Angelica," Shiloh gave her a tired smile. "I'm really glad that you're here because I'm so ready to be off of my feet. How much do you know about meal prep?" she asked, setting down her knife, which, to Susannah's practiced eye, looked like a good quality one.

The killer made a mental note to try to pilfer some decent tools if the opportunity arose.

"Top of my class in culinary school," she shrugged, glancing about the kitchen.

"Wow, awesome," Shiloh nodded. "We try to keep it simple here. We've got fresh veggies that are market castoffs, cuts of meat that the butcher put on sale, and lots of dry goods. You can use anything that we have here, just make sure it's tasty and plentiful. Try to use the tomatoes in something if you can. They're perfectly ripe right now and will start going bad soon," she pointed to a bin of vegetables. "Think you can handle cooking a meal for around ten people?"

"Piece of cake," Susannah assured her, eager to start.

Cooking, like murder, was an art form. Every dish had to be a masterpiece. Taste was paramount and presentation should be flawless. She hated eating at restaurants generally, because either the flavors or textures were off, or the presentation was subpar. Cooking and presenting the meal herself would take care of all of her usual objections, and she'd be able to prepare exactly what she wanted.

"Hey, I'll help too," Devin volunteered. "Just tell me what to do."

"Sure," Susannah forced a smile.

The young man was solidifying her impression of him as a human puppy, cute, clueless and always underfoot.

"Well, I'll let you two take over here, and I'll go out to watch the door," Shiloh waved on her way out of the kitchen.

"So, Angelica, where are you from?" Devin stuck to her like glue as she perused the vegetable bin.

Susannah had correctly guessed that he'd be a chatty Cathy. Great. She would have to definitely work at trying not to let her annoyance and natural aversion to human company show.

"I don't really want to talk about it. It's kind of painful," she murmured, playing to the young man's obvious sensitive side.

"Oh, geez, I'm sorry," he immediately apologized. "I didn't mean to bring up anything bad. I've only been in Chicago for a little while myself. I play violin over on the Mag Mile to try to save up to go to school."

"How's that working out for you?" Susannah asked, not because she cared, but because she was glad that he'd gone along with not talking about her life.

"Well, you know, it's slow, but I have a couple of regular fans who drop money in my case on their way to the train," his head bobbed.

"Great," Susannah hoped that she sounded far more enthusiastic than she felt. "How about carne asada tacos with fresh pico de gallo?" she asked, turning her attention to a much more fascinating subject.

"Sure," Devin agreed, clearly having no idea what she was talking about. "How can I help?"

"Take all of those tomatoes," she pointed. "That onion, the garlic over there, and these three jalapenos, and dice them up as tiny as you can get them," she instructed. "The diced cubes need to be uniform in size, can you do that? Because if you can't, I'll do it myself, while the meat is searing," the look she gave him was uncompromising.

Susannah couldn't stand haphazard food prep, though she couldn't quite justify killing someone over it.

"Ummm...I can do it," Devin looked startled at Susannah's intensity, and she made a Herculean effort to soften her expression. "I'll do a little bit and then check with you on it, okay?" he asked, his eyes wide, like a startled deer.

He was fortunate that there was nothing remarkable about his hair or skin – he'd be all too easy to kill. His lack of arrogance also contributed largely to his continued ability to draw breath.

"That would be great," Susannah nodded, trying to smile without showing her teeth.

She went into the oversized refrigerator and pulled out some cheap cuts of meat, wrapped in butcher paper, taking them back to the butcher block island. After assembling the necessary spices for the savory main dish, she went to work with Shiloh's impressively sharp knife, making a definite plan to come back and steal it later.

The slices of meat that fell from her blade were paper thin and perfectly uniform. She worked with a speed and accuracy that Devin noticed, pausing in his efforts to stare at her, mouth agape. Her mastery with flesh, both animal and human, was legendary.

"Wow, you weren't kidding when you said you were good in the kitchen," he admired her work from across the island.

"Thanks. How's that dicing coming?" she asked pointedly, making an effort to sound at least a bit cordial.

"Let me show you," he offered, picking up his bowl of tomatoes and coming around to her side.

She took a quick glance in the bowl and nodded once.

"Good job," she said, returning her focus to the strands of muscle in front of her.

Devin the violinist had saved his life with his diligence and manner. For now.

"That was amazing, Angelica," Shiloh sighed contentedly, rubbing her swollen belly. "I hope you'll come cook with us again."

"I'd like that," the killer nodded, chewing her last bite.

She'd been pleased with the meal, despite the fact that she'd had to use dried cilantro rather than fresh. It had irked her, but she'd made it work.

"So, where are you staying? Do you have a

place?" Devin asked, drawing fresh ire that she fought to hide.

"I'm working on that," she said shortly, keeping her eyes on her plate.

"Well, if you need a place to crash, there's a building in Old Town that you might want to check out. There are a bunch of artists and musicians who have places there and they let people couch surf. All they ask you to do is just, like, water the plants or walk the dog or whatever," he shrugged. "I can give you some names and addresses if it would help at all."

Hope bloomed within the killer as she imagined the easy pickings that would be at her fingertips in such a place.

"That's really kind of you, Devin. Thank you," she looked him straight in the eye and he dropped his gaze, blushing.

"You're welcome," he grinned, his color deepening.

Shiloh looked from one to the other and smiled, then glanced up as the door opened, admitting a boisterous trio of diners. She rose to greet them, and Susannah stared at Devin until he looked up again.

"Hey, can I get those names and addresses? I really should get going so that I can get settled in," she asked, trying to sound sweet and grateful and not knowing whether or not she was pulling it off successfully.

"Yeah, of course," he stood so quickly that his shirt flipped his fork up into the air. It came down with a clatter on his plate. "Oops, my bad," he blushed again. "I'll be right back."

Susannah was restless, but fortunately she didn't have to wait long. Devin was back in seconds with half a sheet of notebook paper that had names, phone numbers an address and apartment numbers scrawled on it.

"Here you go," he handed it to her, smiling shyly.

"Great thanks," she took it, folded it and put it in her pocket, standing to leave.

"No problem. My number is at the bottom of the sheet, you know, in case you have any questions or whatever," he shoved his hands in the pockets of his worn jeans.

She let that one pass, heading for the door.

"Hey, Angelica?" he called out as she moved through the kitchen, avoiding the new group that had just entered.

"Yeah?" she gritted her teeth, pasting on a smile.

"Are you going to...be around? Like for breakfast or whatever tomorrow?" His huge brown eyes were guileless and innocent, like a sheep that had no idea he was being led to slaughter.

"I'm not sure about breakfast, but I'll be back sometime," she assured him.

"I'm here every Monday through Wednesday," he called out as the door closed behind her.

CHAPTER EIGHT

Life on the run was not something that Tim had been prepared to tolerate. He liked order in his life. Predictability was a good thing. He'd left all semblance of order and predictability when he'd fled from his former home, and it was all Susannah's fault. Susannah, the gifted chef who had harbored deep, dark secrets. His wife. The woman who had actually looked at him and promised to be with him forever.

She was the only woman who had ever loved him, aside from the grandmother who had raised him. His grandmother had passed merely months before he met the serial killer who could cook like no other, so being alone was something with which he was largely unfamiliar, though he'd always been a loner. He was odd. He accepted that. Susannah had seemed to understand and appreciate that, like no one else had ever been able to do.

Timothy Eckels never tried to connect with anyone for the vast majority of his life. The one time that he did think he'd perhaps found a kindred spirit, she happened to be a serial killer. What did that say about him?

Despite his dark thoughts, Tim's mood lifted considerably the further south he went. He was in Florida now, and the palm trees swaying in the tropical breeze did wonders for his state of mind. He relaxed a bit, though his body still went rigid anytime he was remotely close to any sort of law enforcement personnel. He'd nearly dropped his hot pretzel when a mall security guard had passed by, as he hastily ate his meager lunch.

He'd never been to the ocean. He liked it, feeling a sense of awe as he watched the ebb and flow of it. It was a surreal feeling – being out in public, his shoes off, lily-white toes dug in the sugary sand. He'd thought he'd hate it – that it would make him feel unclean - but the freedom that it represented, as well as the warmth and texture of it, actually made him smile...faintly. The sun on his face fed his soul, and he began to think that starting a new life might actually work, though his optimism was more than cautious. He'd believed before. He'd trusted before. And he got screwed, every time. Leaning back against a palm tree, Tim worked at relaxing his shoulders, clearing his mind of all thought.

"Mew!" a plaintive sound, to his immediate left, caught his attention, as he contemplated the light lapping of what passed for waves on the shore.

A tiny striped tabby sidled up and bonked her furry head against his thigh.

"Oh. Hello."

The former mortician reached his hand out tentatively, not wanting to scare the affectionate creature away. He scratched her between the ears, and she nuzzled against his hand, purring.

Relationships with human beings were out of the question at present, and perhaps for the rest of his life, but this non-judgmental little being seemed like she might be a perfect companion. The cat had no idea that he was weird, or introverted, or that one of his greatest joys was preparing the dead, nor did she care. He was warm and willing to pet her. It was all he had to give, and it was everything that she needed.

Eventually, he'd have to start looking for the typical things which defined life in society. A house to rent. A job. Groceries. But for now, watching the ocean and enjoying the motorboat purrs of his new pet were the only items on his agenda.

CHAPTER NINE

Tall, wiry, Leon Cordoba was going to be a very appropriate roommate for Susannah. He had been one of the first names on Devin's list, and five minutes after meeting him, Susannah knew that he'd work out just fine. He was a brooding man who was maybe a few years older than she, and who, more importantly, seemed to have no tolerance for idle conversation. As long as she fed the fish and the birds, and cleaned out the bird cage, she could crash on his couch for however long she needed to. The building that he lived in was quite unique and would lend itself wonderfully to hiding away from the world for as long as she liked.

The entrance to the once-grand apartment building still had the original mosaic tile floor of its heyday, but the tile, like the building itself, showed signs of age and wear. A dark, narrow hall, which was covered in the strange and sometimes beautiful work of its inhabitants, led to a series of narrow doors. Behind each one was a tiny, crumbling apartment, many of which featured only a dorm-sized fridge and a hot plate in the "kitchen", but most of which had floor to ceiling windows and two tiny levels of living space. It was a low-cost haven for artists, musicians and other creative types who wanted to move along in the shadows, unbothered by conventional society.

Leon's bed and television were on the main level, affording Susannah the complete privacy of having her own space in the loft, which could be curtained off from the rest of the apartment. The prospect of sharing living space with another human was rather daunting, but she was under the distinct impression that Leon never ventured near the rickety ladder which led to the loft. It was furnished with a couch, an end table and a lamp, and there was a bar across one end of the small room for hanging clothing.

The entire place was spotless, with the exception of the massive windows, which sported a light grey film of city grime, making even the brightest of sunlight look soft and filtered. It was perfect for Susannah's minimalist preferences. The only drawback to the place was that the apartments didn't have their own bathrooms. There were shared bathrooms scattered throughout the building, and they were, quite frankly, astonishingly disgusting. The thought of showering in the filthy cubicles made her cringe, so she seriously considered slipping into the gym across the street to take care of her necessary cleansing rituals.

Susannah was delighted to learn, after staying in her new place for a couple of days, that Leon Cordoba was never home. Where he went, or what he was doing, she neither knew, nor cared, she just enjoyed the privacy. She had the code to get in the front door, and a key to Leon's place, and had found a back exit into a narrow alley that she could slip into and out of whenever she pleased. It was a good setup, and one that made her hunger for a kill. It also afforded her the time and space that she needed in order to do some research to try and find her husband.

She was tucked away in the loft, her feet curled beneath her, tablet in hand, deeply absorbed in an internet search, when a knock on the front door intruded into her personal time. Leon wasn't home, and it was her policy to never answer the door, so she ignored it. The knock sounded again, followed by a soft, "Angelica? Are you home?"

Devin.

The interruption set her teeth on edge, but she tried to continue to ignore the intrusion.

"Angelica? Hey, it's Devin," he announced.

Her concentration broken, Susannah tossed the tablet aside with a heavy sigh, and climbed down from the loft. Devin began to knock again, and she pulled the door open, startling him.

"Hey! You're home, great," he grinned at her, tucking a strand of hair behind his ear.

Susannah merely stared at him, and his smile dimmed.

"So, like, I hate to bother you," he scratched at his chin, clearly nervous. "I know I'm just showing up out of the blue, but..." he began.

"What is it, Devin?" she prompted, trying to sound polite.

"So...Shiloh went into labor this morning, and there's no one to help me cover lunch at the Co-op. I mean, there's usually only a dozen people or so who come in, and I could do it myself, but people are always kind of in a hurry at lunch time, and so I..." he rambled.

"You want me to come in and help you with

lunch?" she summed it up, unable to take it anymore.

"Oh, yeah, that would be great," he sighed with relief. "I mean, if you can. Even if it's just for a while, because I..."

Seeing that he was about to launch into another potentially lengthy explanation, Susannah interrupted him again.

"Let me just grab my jacket," she shut the door in his face before he could say another word.

"Awesome," she heard his delight filter through the door.

Hands on hips, Susannah surveyed the Co-op kitchen, seeing what the possibilities were, while Devin stared at her like a love-struck teenager.

"So, we always have some frozen veggie burgers on hand. Those are pretty popular at lunch," he volunteered.

Susannah regarded him with thinly disguised disdain.

"Okay, well you can be in charge of the veggie burgers, and I'll make something for people who want real food," she commented, opening the refrigerator.

"Do you not like me?" Devin asked, his expression downcast.

Susannah stared at him, entirely unaccustomed to having someone care how she felt and entirely unprepared to deal with a young man who wore his feelings on his sleeve.

"I don't know you," she looked at him curiously.

"Are you mad because I came and got you today? I just get this vibe that something's wrong."

"Nothing's wrong and I don't dislike you. I take cooking very seriously and when I'm in the kitchen the food is my sole focus," she explained, honestly.

She didn't like people in general, but she wasn't about to tell the emotional human in front of her that. She felt quite certain that it wouldn't take much to make him cry and she had neither the time nor the stomach for his tears.

"Yeah, I picked up on that when we made dinner," a slow smile appeared, and he sighed in relief. "Well, cool. I'm glad we're good, then. So, what are you making?"

"I'm going to see what we've got for meat and make some kind of sandwich on the pumpernickel rolls," she murmured, perusing the contents of the fridge.

"Yeah, the bakery didn't sell them yesterday, so we got them for free. We have potato rolls too, but I usually use those for the burgers."

Susannah didn't answer, she was busily assembling ingredients for an innovative idea that was developing in her mind. Her combinations were sometimes odd, but always delicious, and today would be no exception. She placed a smoked ham, a head of cabbage, a large chunk of swiss cheese, an onion, and a bag of cranberries on the island, drawing a perplexed look from Devin.

"So, uh, is there anything I can do to help?" he asked.

"Take the cabbage and the onion and slice them as thinly as you can. Paper-thin," she instructed, selecting her favorite slicing knife from the rack on the counter.

Much to Susannah's surprise and relief, Devin did what he was told, without comment or question, casting curious looks at her, which she pretended not to notice. The two worked in silence, across the island from each other, and all was well until the back door burst open, admitting a thin young man with a brooding countenance. Susannah's hackles rose, and she studiously ignored the newcomer, who swaggered in with an air that indicated he was looking for trouble.

"Hey, Martin," Devin greeted the new arrival without expression, watching him carefully.

"Hey, yourself," his greeting seemed to mock. "Well, well, well, looks like we have some new blood here," he came up behind Susannah's left shoulder, so close that she could feel his breath stirring the hairs on the back of her neck. Her hand tightened on the knife.

"OW!" Devin shouted in pain, dropped his knife and grabbed the forefinger of his left hand.

Susannah saw blood.

"Step away from the food," she called out, setting her own knife down.

Ironically, one of the benefits of having inflicted so many slices in her lifetime was that she knew how to treat a cut when one happened accidentally. She sprang into action, grabbing a kitchen towel and approaching Devin, whose face had gone deathly pale.

"Look away," she commanded, taking his hand in hers.

She refused to have anyone passing out or vomiting in the kitchen. He complied and she removed his hand from the cut to assess the damage. "It may hurt like hell, but you won't need stitches, so I'm going to need you to suck it up and keep going. Can you do that Devin?" she demanded. "Because if you can't, you need to get out of the kitchen right now."

"I can do it," he said, somewhat breathless, still not looking at the cut.

"Good, where's the first aid kit?"

"In the pantry, top shelf."

"Okay," she wrapped the towel around his finger so that he wouldn't see the blood. "Put pressure on this, and I'll be right back," she ordered, heading for the pantry.

"Well, you are a take-charge kinda woman," Martin drawled, looking Susannah up and down, leaning back against a cabinet, arms crossed. "Need a job, sweet cheeks?" he asked, making it sound suggestive.

"No, she doesn't," Devin barked, surprising Susannah.

She hadn't thought that the delicate violinist had any semblance of a backbone, but the fire in his eyes as he glared at Martin suggested otherwise.

"Wasn't asking you, hippie-boy," Martin's tone was menacing.

Susannah leveled the newcomer with a look, moving to Devin's side.

"Get out of my kitchen," she ordered, ministering to Devin's wound.

"Your kitchen?" Martin didn't move a muscle, seemingly unfazed. "I thought that the whole idea of this free-love, tolerant, socialist place was that it's everybody's kitchen," he challenged.

Susannah finished taping gauze around Devin's finger and went back to her side of the island, while her injured helper put the first aid kit away.

"I wasn't kidding. Get out. We have work to do here, and you're in the way," Susannah moved within reach of her knife, just in case.

"I bet you're a little wildcat in the sack, huh Red?" he sucked his teeth, leering at her.

It confused her when he called her Red at first, then she remembered that she had dyed her hair.

"Hey, man, that's so not appropriate," Devin came back out of the pantry and stood in front of Martin, who shoved him to the side.

Before the miscreant knew what was happening, Susannah deftly grabbed her knife, hooked her arm around his neck, and put the blade to his throat. The strength that she'd honed for the better part of her life made the wiry little man no match for her.

"Whoa," Devin squawked in surprise, his eyes like saucers. "Let's not get crazy here," he held up his hands.

Martin didn't struggle. On the contrary, his leering grin grew wider and he chuckled, not moving within Susannah's iron grasp.

"Don't worry, Junior, she ain't gonna do nothing."

His tone was cocky, but Susannah felt the tremors of adrenaline beneath his skin. She thrilled at the feeling and wanted so, so badly to just slide the blade across his throat then turn him around to watch him bleed out.

"You think not?" she growled softly in his ear, pressing the blade a bit harder against his pale flesh.

"You don't want to play like that, little girl," Martin's warning was shaky, despite his efforts to sound tough.

"You have no idea how I want to play," she whispered, rocking the knife back and forth. "You gonna go quietly, or are we gonna have a problem, here?" she asked.

"Get out of my face, bitch," Martin growled, and Susannah knew that she had won.

Once the epithets began, it meant that fear and prudence had worked their way down into the psyche. She could let go of him without worry now.

She wasn't afraid for herself, but she didn't want Devin to become a victim, unless she was his killer. Susannah released her hold and stepped back, not surprised when Martin whipped around and raised a fist to try and intimidate her.

"Take your best shot," she said mildly, not budging an inch.

With a look of utter fury, Martin dropped his arm and stared at her as he headed for the door, an unsteady smirk playing about his lips. He was posturing and she knew it.

"You'd better watch your back, bitch," he threatened.

"I always do," Susannah smiled a sinister smile, glad that Devin couldn't see her face.

"You'll want to be careful with that guy, Angelica," Devin said quietly, after the door closed behind Martin.

"Why?" Susannah went to the sink to scrub any traces of Martin from her slicing knife.

"He's bad news."

Susannah shrugged. "I've seen his type before. He thinks he's tougher than he actually is."

"He's a pimp," Devin blurted. "When he asked you if you wanted a job, he meant that you could be a prostitute," he blushed.

"That's disgusting," Susannah commented, going back to slicing her ham. "Are you going to be able to work with the bandage on your finger?"

Devin blinked at her for a moment.

"Uh, yeah, I'll just put my glove on over the top of it," he said, seeming dazed.

"Good idea."

"So...you must've had, like, a really hard life, huh?" Devin asked tentatively.

"You have no idea," Susannah muttered.

CHAPTER TEN

Tim wound up in Key West and decided to stay there. He'd found a pie shop near the beach, which specialized in Key Lime Pie. His grandmother had made the best pies known to mankind, and she'd given him a passion for them, so he'd camped out at a bistro table in front of the brilliant green store front, a slab of Key Lime Pie in front of him, the want ads held in one hand, and the stray kitten sleeping in his lap.

The owner of the shop, which featured whimsical mermaids cavorting in a brightly colored mural inside, was a startlingly beautiful woman who was about Tim's age, and when he'd tried to speak to her, he'd failed miserably, barely able to choke out his order. There was just something about her. Not that he was even remotely interested. He'd tried relationships and found that they didn't work for him, so he was done with that phase of his life. He and his still unnamed kitten would be just fine on their own.

While he had more than enough money to live on for the foreseeable future, due to a hefty inheritance from his grandmother, and an almost compulsive saving habit, Tim knew that he needed to have a job. While being unemployed was rather pleasant, it just didn't seem right to fritter away his hours on the beach or playing with his cat. He needed to be productive, and though he wanted to keep a low profile, and couldn't stomach the thought of working within his chosen profession at the moment, he needed the distraction, the purpose. Oddly, for some reason that he couldn't quite fathom, he needed to be needed.

There was a Help Wanted sign in the window of the pie shop, but the thought of being constantly in the presence of the stunning owner filled him with anxiety. He'd be dropping things, spilling and otherwise making a nuisance of himself, despite the fact that his grandmother had passed all of her pie making secrets on to him and he could make a mean pie. He'd exhaust all of his other options before he'd even consider applying. Disgusted with himself for allowing the woman's appearance to throw him off course, Tim pored over the want ads with a singular focus, stopping every now and again for a bite of pie which honestly rivaled his grandmother's, though he'd die before admitting such a thing.

He'd turned his cell phone off days ago, not wanting to be tracked, or found, and had been using a city map to find his way around Key West. He made a list, in order of geographic proximity, of the jobs that he wanted to apply for, and wandered his way around the island, filling out applications and receiving nothing but promises to get back to him. He'd drop his cat at the door when he went inside the various businesses, and she was always there waiting for him when he came out. The tiny striped creature was a constant, reassuring presence in his life now, and he needed as much of that feeling as he could get.

Tired of the tiny room he'd rented at an off-beach motor court, Tim planned to look at homes to rent the next day. Life was happening. He was moving on. Alone. The funny thing was...even though Susannah couldn't possibly have any idea where he was, the former mortician found himself constantly looking over his shoulder. Somehow, he knew that the day would come when she found him.

Guesses as to what she would do when she did danced darkly in his nightmares.

Yeah, he'd lost sleep, lots of it, but he was alive. So far.

Consummate realtor, Josie Applegate, had lived in Key West her entire life, a fact which showed itself profoundly in the tanned skin of her face, and the bleached cloud of her hair. Tim observed, not unkindly, that the texture of her was rather like a well-used leather handbag. She had large white teeth, which regularly presented themselves in a perpetually cheery grin.

Tim, as usual, was soft-spoken and reserved, and she was determined to draw him out while she helped him shop for a rental cottage. The more she chattered, the quieter he got. By the time they got to the last bungalow, a small, charming place set back on the lot which rested on a quiet cul-de-sac, he was more than ready for some alone time. He trailed miserably along behind the petite powerhouse, nodding appreciatively at new kitchen appliances and upgraded flooring, when a flash of red outside the house next door caught his eye.

The woman from the pie shop. Her coppery hair was unmistakable.

"I'll take it," he interrupted Josie's litany of amenities, surprising her.

"This one is at the top of your stated price range, but I think it'll be so worth it," she gushed, a delighted smile lighting her features.

"Yes, I'll take it," Tim repeated, not daring to look out the window again. He didn't want Josie to figure out why he was attracted to this particular...house.

"Well, great! I love decisive clients," she hooked her arm through his and led him to the front door, making him very uncomfortable.

He put up with it. His thoughts were elsewhere... and they haunted him a bit.

CHAPTER ELEVEN

Susannah reserved a huge portion of contempt for men like Martin the Pimp. She found his smug, swaggering demeanor to be positively vile, knowing full well that behind the bravado hid a small man constantly wrestling with self-loathing. Men of his ilk chose to inflict on others the pain that they couldn't handle in themselves, and Susannah would have none of it. She knew when she met him that she'd eventually kill him, because scum like that needed to be purged from humanity. She'd also taken it very personally when he'd come in and leered at her, thinking that he could best her. She was stronger, she was smarter, and she was deadly. He may have inflicted some harm in his world, but Susannah made killing an art form...quite literally.

She had learned, from the ever-chattering Devin,

that Martin lived in her neighborhood. After a few days of skulking around the area, she'd seen him entering a building that was in even worse shape than the one that she lived in. Broken windows that looked like empty eye sockets dotted the building, seeming nastily appropriate for the living quarters of Martin the Pimp, as Susannah referred to him in her mind. She didn't know which of the grimy apartments in the building belonged to her newest choice of victim, but she knew how she planned to find out.

Lolling against the side of Martin's building, Susannah saw a rather rough-looking woman scuffing her way toward the entrance and approached her slowly.

"Hey, do you know Martin?" she asked in a soft voice into which she injected elements of fear and awe.

The woman stared at her, eyes narrowed. "Yeah, why?" she asked.

"I just...uh...I wanted to give him something, and he told me where he lived, but I wrote it on my hand and when I showered, it wasn't there anymore," Susannah lied, holding up her empty palm toward the woman.

"He likes 'em dumb, that's for sure," the prostitute rolled her eyes. "It's 4A, but he ain't there right now," she announced, turning back toward the building.

"He's not?"

"No, he don't never come back to his house 'til after eight, didn't he tell you that? And he don't like bitches waitin' for him on his doorstep," she warned.

"I...I don't remember, I was really drunk when we...talked," Susannah feigned embarrassment.

"When you...talked. Right," the woman shook her head. "Look, honey. You ain't nothing special. He's gonna use your ass up turning tricks and throw you away, just like the rest of us. So, if you got some wild idea about being his bitch, you might as well give that shit up right now," the weary hooker turned and walked away.

"Uh, okay...thanks," Susannah scuttled back to the side of the building, slipped down the alley and headed toward home with a sunny smile on her face.

Tonight was going to be fun.

It felt so good to prepare for her night out with Martin. She dressed in black clothing, making sure that her pants were form-hugging, and her long-sleeved knit shirt was low cut. She pulled a black beanie over her short reddish locks, feeling thrill after delicious thrill jolt through her as she antici-pated the glorious bloodletting that was soon to be hers. She tried as best as she could to keep her excitement focused on the blood and power. Other urges were too problematic to think about at the moment.

Her Timmy was paunchy, pasty and bespectacled, with thinning hair and a definite dad-bod. He spoke softly, rarely showed emotion in any form, and was hardly ever disagreeable. Mild-mannered though he may have been, he'd been more than able to take care of her in the afterglow of murder. She hadn't had sex since a few days before her arrest, and the need for her husband continued to burn deep inside, but she was determined to ignore it for now, and focus on the task at hand.

Lurking in the shadows next to Martin's building, a fierce hunger grew within Susannah. She trembled with anticipation just thinking about the blade of the ultra-sharp meat cleaver that she'd pilfered from the Co-op, slicing neatly through the pimp's pale flesh. She'd stashed the cleaver in Angelica's backpack, along with a pair of tough kitchen shears, a utility knife that Leon had tucked in a drawer, a box of plastic baggies for her souvenirs, a roll of duct tape, and a few pairs of plastic gloves from the Co-op's kitchen. The pack was slung casually over one shoulder, the instruments within it wrapped in t-shirts so that they made no noise when she moved. She was resolved to wait as long as she needed to, but fortunately, she didn't have to wait long. Just as the worn-out tart had predicted, Martin came strutting toward his building, right after eight o'clock. Darkness shrouded the city, and her prey was alone.

"Let's play," Susannah whispered, already making plans for the souvenirs that she would slice from that pale, white skin.

"What the fuck?" Martin shouted, when Susannah knocked on his door a few minutes after he got home. "Can I even get a fucking beer without someone bugging me?" he ranted, yanking open the door to a deceptively sweet-looking Susannah.

Surprise overshadowed his anger and he stared at her, confused.

"What the hell do you want?" he asked, blood-shot eyes narrowed, clearly recognizing her.

"I...uh...I think we got off to a bad start," she smiled in a manner that she hoped came off as being coy, rather than predatory. Putting one hand up to her neck, she ran a finger along the edge of her shirt, and trailed it down toward her cleavage, acting as though it was an unconscious gesture. "You came in on a bad day...I wasn't exactly myself," she shrugged, biting her lip as she'd seen other women do when they were trying to manipulate a man.

"Bout time you came to your senses, sweetheart," the leering grin was back.

"Yeah, I was kinda rude."

"You pull that shit again and I will fuck you up, you understand me?" Martin demanded with a forced benevolent smile, grabbing her by the chin and giving her head a little shake.

She envisioned opening her mouth, tipping her head down and biting through a vital vein in his wrist, causing rich jets of blood to gush from him, spurting onto her face. This made her smile, which he apparently took as a form of encouragement.

"Do you have time to go for a walk with me?" Susannah asked. "I mean, I'm sure you're probably busy and all, but there are some things that I'd like to talk to you about and...show you," she touched the pink tip of her tongue to her top lip, then slipped it back inside.

"Oh, believe me baby, I've got some things that I want to show you," he nodded, a malignant smile on his face. "Why don't you just come inside? I'm not exactly a nature guy," he opened the door wider and held out his hands.

Susannah couldn't help but notice the evidence

of his intentions bulging under his sweatpants, and despite her unconditional loathing of this particular subhuman, she felt a slight tingle at the sight.

"It'll just be a short walk," she promised, making a heroic effort to sound eager and excited. "I really want to show you this...thing," she smiled shyly and dropped her eyes, trying not to burst into manic giggles at her over-the-top performance. He bought it.

"Alright," he nodded. "Gonna make me wait for it. I get how you bitches work, but no worries. You're gonna make it worth the wait," he commented darkly. "I'll get my phone and keys, hang on," he said, closing the door most of the way, while Susannah stood on his doorstep.

"So, how'd you find me, anyhow?" Martin asked, strolling beside Susannah down an alley, hands in his pockets.

"There's nothing a determined woman can't do," she smiled sadistically.

"Damn right. I tell those bitches that all the time when they start slacking," he cracked himself up.

"Do they find that motivational?" Susannah

rolled her eyes, thankful that he couldn't see her expressions in the darkness of the alley.

"Motivational, yeah, that's it," he laughed again, his angry mood seemingly gone. "Where the hell we going, anyway?"

"Just a few more blocks," Susannah promised, hooking a thumb in her pants pocket and allowing her fingers to dangle quite near her crotch, drawing his attention there.

She'd done her homework. In an alley a few blocks away, there was a hidden alcove between garages where no one in the surrounding town-homes could see what might be happening. There were two tall, plastic, recycling containers in the alcove, which she had moved about three feet from the back wall. Recycling didn't get collected in this neighborhood until Thursday, so she figured that Martin's corpse wouldn't be discovered until then.

Susannah had stashed a baseball bat between the containers and planned to use it for her date with Martin.

"Why you got gloves on?" Martin asked, pointing at her thin black leather gloves.

She'd brought plastic gloves for when she dove into the messy work of killing and collecting souvenirs, but she didn't want to leave prints on the bat when she got started, so she'd acquired the black leather gloves from a female executive who'd been so busy on a phone call that she hadn't felt the killer lifting them out of her coat pocket.

"It's cold out here," she shrugged. "Aren't you cold?"

"Nah, I'm pretty hot," he nudged her with his elbow.

"Lucky you," she grinned, mentally rolling her eyes at the fact that he hadn't even noticed that she wasn't wearing a coat, and relishing the thought of what she was about to do to him. "Well, here we are," she stopped in front of the alcove.

"What's here?" Martin frowned.

"The place where I'm gonna have more fun than I've had in quite a while. Come with me," she purred, slipping into the shadows.

He followed her into the dark space, which measured roughly seven feet by ten feet.

"You gonna show me something now?" he asked, grabbing his crotch suggestively.

"Yeah, I am," she said, her voice husky with lust. Bloodlust. "Look back here," she stood in front of the containers and pointed behind them.

"Back there?" he frowned. "I see everything I

need to see right here," his eyes assaulted her, raking up and down her body.

She hated it, but felt oddly titillated at the same time. It had to be the promise of blood that was tripping her trigger.

"Yeah. You're gonna like it. I've got something special set up for you," she smiled, her voice trembling slightly.

"Sounds like I'm not the only one who's hot around here," he smirked. "What am I looking for?" He went around the side of the containers and squinted into the darkness behind them. "Is that a sleeping bag?" his tone changed dramatically, from skeptical to driven.

"Yeah, there's a candle down there too. Light it with this," Susannah could hardly keep the excitement out of her voice as she tossed him a small cigarette lighter, then reached for the bat.

"Baby girl wants some romance, huh? You better give it to me good after all this," Martin grumbled, crouching. "Hey, it's dark, I don't see a candle..."

His sentence was brutally cut off as Susannah swung the baseball bat as hard as she could, nailing him in the left temple. She was glad that, instead of crying out, he just sort of grunted. Putting a hand to his bleeding head and blinking slowly, he turned and looked at her, his mouth gaping. Before Martin had the presence of mind to raise his hands in defense, she swung again, connecting with the same spot, crushing his fingers, blood spattering on the bat and on the wall next to him. He crumpled limply to the ground – now the real fun could begin.

Moving toward him, smelling the blood and loving it, Susannah froze in place. A sound. A screen door slammed shut on the back of one of the townhomes next to the recycling area.

"C'mon Rocko, do your thing, we've gotta get going," she heard an irritated male say.

Susannah's heart began to pound, and she glanced down at the fallen pimp, who hadn't yet begun to stir. He'd be regaining consciousness at any moment – she didn't have time to waste - but as she stood, listening, she heard another sound. A snuffling, and wuffling, coming from the other side of the enclosure. A dog. Shit.

Controlling her breathing, Susannah's eyes darted about, looking desperately for an escape route. If the dog's owner came out to see what the dog was sniffing at, she could run, but she'd still be seen. Martin the Pimp would be found and cared for, and he'd know what she'd done. She'd be a marked woman, even if she managed to get away now.

The dog started growling, then immediately began barking like crazy. Susannah cursed under her breath, and looked for a hiding spot, but there was none to be found. It sounded like a little dog, which was good, and it was still on the other side of the enclosure, which was even better, but it could dart around the side at any second. Just as that horrific thought crossed her mind, Martin's hand twitched. SHIT!

"Rocko! Shut up and get back here!" the now-angry dog owner snapped.

Susannah felt a glimmer of hope, then...

"Don't make me come get you, stupid dog!" the owner threatened.

Susannah had planned to kill one nasty man, that's it, and he showed signs of reviving, which could be terribly problematic. Now, she might be faced with killing two men and a dog. Not only had she not prepared for that, if she had to kill the guy with the dog, he would be missed, which would prompt an investigation.

Still crouched, not knowing what to do, she heard the thud of impatient footsteps pounding toward her, over the din of the yapping animal. Her nerve endings fried, she took a deep breath and prepared to do battle. Two things happened at once.

A hand shot out from where Martin lay, grabbing her around the ankle, and the barking ceased with a single yelp.

"Come on, stupid dog," the voice growled, moving away from her.

She didn't have time to breathe a sigh of relief, however. Martin groaned and rolled over onto his side. Still holding the bat, she drove it down on his temple again, needing to silence him for a bit longer, until the abusive townhome owner was safely tucked back inside.

Humiliation would be a key part of Martin's death for Susannah. He treated her and apparently all women as though they were worthless, so the more she could embarrass him and make him feel small and powerless, the better. In order to accomplish that, she had to have him naked. Moving quickly, she peeled off her leather gloves, threw them in the backpack, and snapped on a pair of plastic ones. Grabbing the duct tape, she pulled Martin's long-sleeved thermal shirt off over his head, duct-taping his wrists together. His hi-top shoes were perpetually untied, and he wore no socks, so it was easy enough to take them off and toss them in the recycling bin. Thankful that he'd worn sweatpants, she pulled them and his thin cotton boxers down, casting them aside, on top of his shirt. She bound his ankles and he started to come around, groaning softly.

"Can't have that," Susannah murmured, sitting astride him and placing a six inch strip of duct tape over his mouth.

Martin was having a rough time regaining consciousness, after the latest blow of the bat, and now that he was trussed up like a turkey, she hoped he wouldn't take too long to come around. She wanted to get to the good stuff. While he blinked slowly, rolling his head from side to side, she took the opportunity to climb off of him and study the tattoos she'd noticed as she was disrobing him. Most of them were garden-variety tattoos, put in place to show others how tough he was, but she happened upon one, just inside his right bicep, that caused a bright red miasma of fury to rise up within her. When she saw that tattoo, she realized that tonight would be no ordinary kill. She would do everything in her power to make it the most painful, psychologically abhorrent thing that any human could ever experience, and she would glory in it.

"Nazi scumbag," she whispered, staring, revolted, at the swastika emblazoned upon the piece of human trash below her.

Susannah despised men who exerted their power and authority over others, and when she'd learned about Hitler and the Third Reich in history class, she'd nearly come unglued. The man was the epitome of evil male dominance, and anyone who admired him had to die, it was just that simple.

The titillated killer climbed back on top of Martin's naked body just as he was starting to regain consciousness. She found it utterly fascinating that, unlike most people, who woke to reality with fear and bewilderment, Martin was simply pissed beyond belief. Dark fury rose in his eyes and he immediately began to struggle, which was no easy task for someone who was bound, hand and foot, with a serial killer perched on his abdomen.

"Quit," Susannah insisted, giving him a quick jab in the thigh with a utility knife. It felt so good to feel the firmness of flesh beneath her blade again.

Martin's struggles grew more desperate. He thrashed and flailed below her while she calmly squeezed her thighs together around him, so that he couldn't buck her off as she withdrew the rest of her tools from the backpack. In the midst of his violent thrashing, Martin slammed his head on the concrete below him, making his world go temporarily grey again. He stilled, on the verge of passing out.

"That was dumb, Martin," Susannah observed, taking a sightline down the blade of the meat cleaver, turning it from side to side in the faint glow of the security lights above the surrounding garages.

Martin pulled his knees up, trying to get Susannah off of him, and she jabbed him in the thigh again.

"You'll want to stop that," she said mildly, as his body began to shake violently from shock and pain.

"Awww...did that hurt, little Nazi?" she cooed. "If not, I'll do better next time," she promised, fire in her eyes. "You know, I thought that you were just a little insecure, and that's why you were such a loser. You were posturing because you felt that you had something to prove. Now I know that you really believed the putrid filth spewed by the most evil man on the planet, and that, dear Martin, is going to make your death far worse than it would've been, had you merely been a poser," she promised him, putting her face very close to his.

So close that her breath fanned his face. She could feel the heat of fear rolling off of him in waves, yet he refused to give in. He cursed and hurled epithets from behind the duct tape.

"The first thing that I'm going to have to get rid of is that nasty swastika," she waggled the utility knife in front of Martin's eyes, and his chest heaved up and down, his breath coming in frenzied gasps through his nose. He screamed and screamed through his nose, not out of his pain, but out of anger.

"Stop it," she brought the handle of the knife down between his eyes, hard, and he went still, seeming dazed. "You're not going to be allowed to scream, or pass out. You're going to stay awake and take this like a man."

Martin's hands were pinned under her bottom, his fingers scrabbling madly against her buttocks.

"Stay still or I burst an eyeball," Susannah raised an eyebrow at him, holding the utility knife over his left eye. His movements ceased.

She pulled the skin of his bicep hard to the right, so she could access the swastika, which was about an inch square.

"This is going to hurt," she promised, grinning down at him. "And I want you to feel every bit of it."

Susannah plunged the utility knife into the skin of Martin's bicep, sinking it in less than a quarter of an inch. If she went any deeper than that, the tattoos tended to take too long to dry out in the oven. The Nazi wannabe screamed once, as she started carefully harvesting the tattoo, separating skin from the tissue beneath it, then passed out. He came to again when she lifted the perfect square free. She dangled the flap of skin over his face, swiping it across his nose, leaving a trail of blood. Tears rolled down the sides of his head into his ears, and he moaned through his nose.

"You know what?" she said pensively. "This is the worst tattoo ever. I don't even want it. Hmm...what should I do with it?" she toyed with him while he convulsed in pain.

Pretending to sniff it, she made a face. "This thing stinks," she taunted. "Wanna smell it, Nazi boy?" she smiled a slow, torturous grin.

Holding it directly over his face, Susannah began to roll the small square of skin into a tight cylinder, squeezing droplets of blood out of it, which spattered on Martin's forehead.

"Sniff on this, Martin," she suppressed a wicked giggle, and stuffed the cylinder of skin up his left nostril, shutting off half of his breathing capability. She would have preferred to make him eat it, but she couldn't risk taking the tape off and letting him scream. There was also the odd chance that he might vomit once the tattoo was forced into his mouth, and she didn't have the time or inclination to deal with that mess.

His eyes went wide as the lack of air began to terrify him. A horrific series of sounds ground out of his throat as stray dribbles of blood from the tattoo made their way into his sinuses.

"You do realize that if you vomit while your mouth is duct-taped that you'll drown, right? And that would be no fun, so come on, just play along like a good little Nazi pimp," she patted his cheek with her gloved hand.

"You really took the coward's way out, getting your rancid little tattoo where it would always be covered so that no one could see it," she chastised him, idly watching the blood ooze from his arm, dribbling a bit faster with the rhythm of his galloping heartbeat. "That just won't do, Martin," she brought the tip of the blade to his forehead and the tremors in his body increased. She could hear his teeth clacking together below the tape, and found the sound somehow comforting. "Your beliefs are going to be on your forehead, for all the world to see," she promised lightly, making her first slice.

CHAPTER TWELVE

When SubLime Sweets owner, Marilyn Hayes, returned home after an incredibly busy day, she was shocked, and a little bit sad, to see that there was a furniture delivery truck in front of the cottage next door that her dear friend Madge had recently vacated. The realization that someone was moving in already made her heart ache. It seemed as though life just plowed right along, whether one was ready for change or not. She assumed that the new tenant must have been taking a break or something, because, while there were boxes of what looked like newly purchased items filling the open garage, along with a bit of shrink-wrapped furniture, there was no sign of the new occupant. Marilyn hoped that whoever it was would turn out to be as lovely as Madge had been. She made a mental note to take a pie over, either later this evening or tomorrow, to welcome the newcomer and introduce herself.

Deciding to drown her sorrows in something entirely unhealthy, she ordered a combination pizza with extra cheese. Opening a decent bottle of Pinot Noir to accompany her feast, Marilyn poured herself a generous measure, sunk into her gloriously over-stuffed couch, and started flipping through the Netflix selection screens, wanting nothing more than to zone out to a good movie. Skipping the Adventure and Drama categories, she went straight to Romantic Comedies, looking to live vicariously through the antics of onscreen relationships. She didn't have the stamina to watch anything that required more than a bare minimum of thought, so light and sweet seemed to be the logical choice.

The doorbell rang a mere ten minutes after she ordered, and Marilyn looked at her watch, astonished and impressed by the extreme efficiency of her pizza delivery service. Tossing the remote onto the couch, without yet having selected a movie, she went to the door and opened it, surprised that the frumpy, bespectacled man standing on the other side of it didn't have a pizza in his hands.

"Hello," Marilyn smiled, confused.

"Hi," the somewhat timid, sandy-haired man

with horn-rimmed glasses replied. "I'm your new neighbor, Tim Eckels," he stuck out his hand and she shook it.

His grip was firm, but his flesh felt oddly clammy and soft. She resisted the impulse to wipe her palm down the leg of her jeans when he let go.

"Oh! Well, welcome to the neighborhood."

She smiled, thinking that his timing couldn't have been worse. Her pizza was on the way, she was tired, and she just wanted to kick back on the couch and chill.

"Thanks. I hate to be a bother, but do you happen to have any twine? There are some bushes in the backyard that are a little top-heavy, so I wanted to give them some support, and my garden supplies are all packed away in a box somewhere," he explained, glancing about as though he had forgotten something.

The twitchy movement of his eyes unsettled her a bit, and she'd never heard of tying up plants with twine before, but she nodded nonetheless.

"Sure, hang on just a second, I'll be right back," she promised, leaving the front door open with Tim standing awkwardly on the porch.

Marilyn went to the kitchen drawer that held office and craft supplies, and pulled out a ball of twine, then went to the refrigerator to retrieve the pie that she had been planning to take to the new neighbor, figuring that since he was here, she could just give it to him now, and save herself a trip next door later. She almost always had a spare pie or two in her fridge – occupational hazard. She and Tiara practically lived on Key Lime pie.

"Great. Thanks so much," Tim said, accepting the twine and the pie. "This'll be dinner for me," he shrugged. "It's been a long day."

"I bet," Marilyn replied, putting on what she hoped was a suitably sympathetic face. "Good luck getting settled," she smiled brightly.

The pizza truck rolled around the corner, pulling into her driveway. She had to get rid of her neighbor quickly, before he noticed the pizza delivery and gave her a pitiful look, indicating a desire to share her dinner.

"I'll check on you in the morning to see how things are coming along," she promised with a wave, and shut the door before he could reply.

She leaned against it, feeling like a heel, but wishing that she had said something to get rid of her nice, but slightly creepy, neighbor without having to promise to see him again.

"Well, good morning to you too, my darling daughter," Marilyn teased, giving the beautiful blonde a quick kiss on the cheek.

"Sleep well?"

"Yes, I did, thank you. Apparently, an angel of mercy covered me up with a blanket last night and I stayed on the couch the entire time," she winked.

"Do angels get bonuses?" Tiara raised her eyebrows hopefully.

"If they find good candidates for our position they do," Marilyn replied, heading to the SubLime Sweets' kitchen.

She spent the morning perfecting a Key Lime mousse that was out of this world, and had more than enough time to review resumes at length before meeting with the first candidate.

Just before closing, after the last job applicant was ushered out, Tiara poked her head into the office.

"One more to go, and then we can call it a day," she advised.

"I thought we were done," Marilyn sighed.

"Be brave, little camper, one more interview won't kill you. I'll send him in."

"Fine," she grimaced, wanting nothing more than to pack up and go home for the day.

She rolled her head from shoulder to shoulder, wincing at the crackling sound that the simple act produced. The sound of stress, she should be accustomed to it by now.

"Hello," a mild, familiar voice startled her.

"Mr. Eckels...what can I do for you?" Marilyn asked warily, wondering how her odd neighbor had managed to find out where she worked. She hadn't noticed when he'd stopped in before, Tiara had waited on him.

"I...uh, here's my resume," he said, handing it to her and taking a seat across the desk from her without being invited in.

"I'm afraid I don't understand," she replied, not looking at the paper in her hand.

"My resume...I'm here to apply for the position you advertised," he blinked at her owlishly from behind his glasses.

He'd tried his luck with getting another position, but apparently no one in Key West wanted to hire an out-of-work mortician.

"Oh! Uh...well, okay then. Give me a moment to review your information," she said, looking down at the paper, but entirely unable to focus on the words.

"I mean...ummm...tell me about your background," she floundered, totally off-balance and glad that he'd left the door open.

"I've worked as a mortician for several years, but baking has always been my hobby. When I tasted your pie, then saw in the local classifieds that you had an opening, I just had to apply. It seems that your standards of excellence are on par with mine, which would make me a beneficial and logical addition to your staff," he smiled faintly, the expression looking somehow unnatural on him.

"A mortician...how...interesting," Marilyn tried not to go green at the gills at the thought.

"Yes, well, it's certainly not a career for everyone, but the work can be rewarding," Tim blinked at her again.

"I'm sure," she replied, suppressing a shudder. "Well, I have a lot of resumes to review, but if yours is selected, I'll be sure to let you know. Thanks for stopping by."

She stood, trying to politely dismiss the odd, pale man.

"Don't you want to ask me any questions?" his eyes narrowed. "I'm sure you wouldn't want to give anyone the impression that you discriminate, based upon gender or past occupation, now would you?"

he smirked, strange green eyes gleaming behind his glasses in a way that struck Marilyn as sinister.

"I resent your implication, Mr. Eckels. You came in here at the last moment, without an appointment, and I not only agreed to look at your resume after a full day of interviewing, but stayed after closing to talk with you. I told you that I have a lot of resumes to review, and yours will be held to the same standards as all of the others."

Tim Eckels rose from his chair slowly, never breaking eye contact. He stood staring down at her for what seemed an awkwardly long time. A sheen of sweat broke out along Marilyn's upper lip, but she refused to let him have the upper hand, and stared right back.

"Thank you for your time, Ms. Hayes," he said in a tone that seemed somehow menacing. "I'll look forward to hearing from you."

He turned on his heel and left without another word, leaving her staring after him, chilled to the bone.

Tim berated himself the entire way home, for the manner in which he'd treated Marilyn Hayes. She was such an attractive woman that he'd studied old movies to try to figure out how to interact with her, without making a fool of himself. And he'd failed. Miserably. Apparently, only Clark Gable could successfully pull off an effective alpha male routine.

On his way home from SubLime Sweets, Tim passed by the lifeless form of a stray dog that had wandered into the wrong lane of traffic, and the pitiful sight gave him an idea. He pulled to the side of the road and got out of his car, thankful that there was almost no traffic. Approaching the stiffening mutt, he knelt down beside it.

"Oh, doggie," he murmured, seeing the drying trickle of blood that adhered the animal's head to the pavement below it. "Poor doggie," he whispered, sliding his hands under the dog.

Scooping up the body, he carried it to his car and laid it on top of a tarp in the trunk to take it home with him. He hadn't been having much luck with finding a job, and he desperately needed a hobby, so he figured he might as well do something that would help him keep his preparation techniques fresh. He dabbled a bit in taxidermy in the past, and it had helped him hone his already impressive reconstruction work to an art form. Supplies could be obtained easily enough, and it would help pass the time.

His fingers itched to bring beauty back to the partially mangled pup. He'd beautifully prepared the dead for years, it was a skill he didn't want to lose. He'd go back to his work with the dead, professionally, eventually. Perhaps after his murderous wife was behind bars and he no longer had to fear her finding him.

There was a workbench in the garage that would be perfect for certain aspects of his hobby, but until his supplies came in, he stashed the body of the dog in an oversized freezer, which had been left by the cottage's owner. He was sure she wouldn't mind.

Puttering around in the kitchen to see what he'd make for his dinner, Tim was startled when his phone rang. No one ever called him. Not even telemarketers, thankfully. The only reason he left the phone on was in case his realtor needed to get in touch with him about the sale of his home. He pulled the phone out of his pocket and glanced at the screen.

Unknown.

A feeling of dread unfurled in the pit of his empty stomach, and he swallowed, his throat making a dry click. He set the phone on the counter, and hit Accept, then the speakerphone symbol. He didn't say hello. He didn't make a sound. He just listened.

No one spoke.

He listened hard. For any sound. Any clue as to who was on the other end of the line.

Nothing.

Then a click. Dial tone.

Trembling slightly, Tim picked up the phone as though it had a contagious disease and slipped it back into his pocket. He didn't want to know who had called. He wanted to believe that it had just been something automated to respond only when it heard a voice. He wanted to believe that. But he didn't. He knew. Somehow, he knew. It was her. It was Susannah...and she was looking for him.

CHAPTER THIRTEEN

Susannah hung up the phone. All she'd wanted was to hear his voice, and he'd denied her that. He'd answered the phone with silence. That was so like him. To wait, to listen. To withhold even the sound of his voice from her. Punishing her. How dare he?

The thrill of killing Martin the Pimp still thrummed through her veins. It had satiated one hunger, but had profoundly ignited another. Married life had worked well for her, in that, when she came home from a kill, her need writhing within her like a coiled serpent, Tim had dutifully taken care of her most primal urges. Sex was almost never something that he initiated, but he seemed perfectly willing to rise to the occasion when Susannah had demands. And now, there was no Tim. He'd disappeared. The frustration and yearning that bubbled within her were like a time bomb. At some point, she'd have to seek release, which meant interacting with another human being, something that she was loathe to do.

A knock sounded at the front door and she could've screamed. She prowled about the apartment like a restless animal. Whoever was on the other side of that door might as well have been asking to be admitted to a lion's den. Susannah was not a happy serial killer at the moment, she was a horny one, and that pissed her off.

"Hey, Angelica...?" another knock and a tentative inquiry.

Devin.

Susannah stopped her pacing and stood stock-still, a wicked smile curling her lips upward. He was young, he had great hair, and his youthful skin was smooth as silk. Her thoughts lingered on his slim hips, perpetually clad in soft, worn denim.

"You'll do," she whispered, going to the door.

"Wow. Angelica, that was...I can't even describe it," Devin panted, lying on his back, drenched in sweat. "You're like...ferocious, but in a good way," he flopped an arm over his eyes, recovering. "I mean, I thought you might not even like me at all, and then..."

Susannah cut off the incessant flow of words by placing a fingertip on the starstruck lad's lips. She liked the feel of them. They might make good souvenirs if she decided to kill him, and if he kept talking, she just might.

"Sorry, was I talking too much?" his lips moved beneath her finger, and she pressed down harder, feeling the rigidity of his teeth beneath the tender skin. "Ow."

"Don't talk," she drawled, mellowed at last.

"Sorry, I..." he began again.

"And stop apologizing."

At his next 'sorry,' she squeezed his mouth with one hand, silencing him, then let him go. Rising from the thin mattress of the foldout couch, she padded, naked and unashamed, to where his clothes were strewn about on the floor. She picked them up and held them out to him.

"Are you mad or something?" he asked, his doe-eyed gaze annoying the hell out of her.

"No," she said simply, shaking the clothing to compel him to get out of bed.

"Are you sure? Because if I said or did

anything..." he rose and hurried to her, his hand reaching out to try and touch her face.

Susannah stepped deftly to the side, dodging him, and thrust the clothing into his hands.

"Look, don't make this weird, okay?" she said, as nicely as she could manage.

The young man had served his purpose and now she wanted to be alone. She had to find Tim. While Devin had been able to serve as a substitute for now, she knew that if she spent any significant time around him, he'd end up dead, and by her measure, he didn't deserve that. She didn't kill people who annoyed her. She almost always killed people who were domineering, arrogant pricks, and she wanted to keep it that way.

"You're right," he hung his head. "I'm sorry."

"Stop apologizing," she snapped.

"Yeah, okay," his head bobbed. "So, we're good then?" he asked, the innocent hope in his eyes turning her stomach a bit.

"Yeah, we're good," she attempted a smile, and he bought it.

She could tell by the sudden glow on his face as he shrugged back into his clothing.

"Good," he grinned. "Oh, by the way, I came by to ask you...do you think you could come cook at the

Co-op tomorrow? There's some kind of special thing going on, and so far, it looks like I'm the only one who's going to be there to cook."

Susannah thought about it. She could do some research tonight to try and track down her husband. It wouldn't kill her to spend some time cooking. Her thoughts seemed to have a special clarity when she was wielding a knife, and she could always do more research after she finished at the Co-op. Besides, now that she'd had a good kill and a bit of sexual satisfaction, she was starving. She'd grab a snack now, and reserve the bulk of her appetite for tomorrow.

"Sure, I can do that," she agreed, trotting down the stairs to the main floor, with Devin at her heels like a golden retriever.

"Great. I won't be weird, I promise. No one will know," he assured her earnestly.

"Know what?" she decided to toy with him.

Devin blushed from his neck to his rather large ears.

"About…like…us, you know," he gave her a goofy smile.

Susannah stared at him.

"Devin, there is no us. You need to understand that."

"What? But...well, I mean, I just thought..." he stammered, turning an even darker shade of red.

"It's fine. There's nothing wrong at all with two people using each other to get off. But that doesn't have to have any deeper meaning. I'm not in a position to have a relationship right now, so don't even think along those lines, got it?"

"Oh. Well, yeah, sure," he nodded, not sounding at all certain.

"Good. I'll see you tomorrow," Susannah opened the door.

"So...do you think that..."

"Yes, Devin, we'll probably do it again, but don't bug me about it."

His relief was almost palpable.

"Okay," the smile was back. "See you tomorrow."

He ducked out and was gone. Mercifully.

"So, what's the special occasion, anyway?" Susannah asked, rolling up her sleeves and donning gloves.

"I'm not really sure," Devin frowned. "There's gonna be like a news crew and like some kind of government people. They're doing a story on people who are just getting together to do their own thing to help people eat and find places to stay and stuff. I guess independent free-spirits are cool now," he chuckled at his own joke, not noticing that Susannah had gone deathly pale.

"I'm not going to do that," she said woodenly.

Devin finally noticed her reaction.

"Oh, hey, don't worry about it. We don't have to say anything, or do anything special. Shiloh is going to be interviewed. We just have to feed people who come in, like usual," he reassured her.

"No. I'm definitely not doing this," Susannah shook her head and began pulling off her gloves.

"Angelica, wait. You can't bail on me," Devin pleaded. "I'm the only one here and I definitely can't handle the lunch rush by myself. Please, Angelica, don't."

He was begging now, which nauseated her. He reminded her of one of her victims, but he didn't have nearly the motivation to be so pathetic. She considered her options. She was starving and had been looking forward to making a decent meal all morning, but...government officials and reporters? She could be opening herself up to discovery and she definitely couldn't risk that.

"I can't," she shook her head.

"At least help me prep," he implored, his eyes wide with fright.

He looked like a startled deer, ripe for killing.

"Seriously, you can leave after we figure out what we're going to cook. I got some sausage and kale from the market this morning, and I have no idea what to do with it."

His voice got higher and his words flowed faster. He was clearly on the verge of panic. Susannah sighed.

"Do we have potatoes?" she asked, not looking at him.

She didn't want him to see the traces of fear in her eyes.

"Yes."

"Fine. I'll help you do prep, and then I'm gone," she muttered.

"Are you okay?" he asked, puzzled, but relieved.

"No, I don't feel well, so I'll be leaving as soon as we're done with prep."

It was true, she didn't feel well. The thought of TV cameras turned her stomach, and she was beginning to feel faint from hunger.

"You're the best," Devin smiled at her. "I'm really sorry that you're not feeling good. Is there anything I can do?"

"Slice potatoes an eighth of an inch thick, then do the same with the onions," she directed, knowing that once things got rolling in the kitchen, she'd feel better.

"Can do. What are we making?"

"Zuppa Toscana."

"Uh...what's that?"

"Italian soup," Susannah sighed.

Were they teaching nothing in school these days?

"Cool," Devin nodded.

The two of them went at their tasks in companionable silence, Susannah's knife flashing as she worked out her anxieties. She'd just finished adding the ingredients for the base of the dish into an oversized stock pot, when they heard a commotion in the dining room that could only mean the arrival of the news crew. Susannah's head snapped up, and her eyes looked, briefly, like those of a trapped animal.

"I really have to go," she announced, tearing off her gloves and tossing her apron on the counter.

"Angelica, wait," Devin called out. "I don't know how to cook this," he protested.

"Just throw it all in the pot and let it simmer for half an hour," she tossed over her shoulder on her way out the door.

In her haste to dash down the back steps, she nearly collided with a large man in uniform.

"Whoa there, little lady," he grinned, catching her by the upper arms to steady her.

"Sorry," she muttered, shifting to the side to try to pass.

"You one of the cooks? I'm Willie Burton, Chief of Police. It's a wonderful thing you've got going here. Neighbors helping neighbors, we need more of that," he nodded sagely. "What's your name?"

"I'm sorry, I really have to go," Susannah tried to smile, but her face felt frozen.

"You okay?" the Chief asked, then frowned. "Hey, you look familiar," he observed.

Susannah's heart beat wildly in her chest. She knew that, as a fugitive, her Wanted picture might very well be hanging in every police station across the country.

"I just have one of those faces," she barked out a laugh, but even to her own ears it sounded forced, false.

"Mmhmm..." the Chief continued to stare, though Susannah avoided his eyes. "The news crew should be set up inside by now. Why don't you show me the kitchen before you go?" he asked pleasantly.

Susannah couldn't read him. Was he actually

being polite, or was he trying to trap her? Her panic made her blind to his intentions. Typically, she could read people like a book, particularly powerful men. They tended to be among the most basic type of life forms, but Chief Burton was inscrutable.

"I'm sorry, I'm not feeling well, I really have to go. I shouldn't be handling food," Susannah ducked her head and slipped past the Chief and three other people who had been standing behind him.

She could feel the weight of his gaze as she trudged down the alley, hoping like hell that he didn't have anyone follow her. If he asked Devin any questions, the innocent young man would probably tell him anything he wanted to know. Including the fact that she was new in town, and that she knew her way around knives. And maybe the Chief would suddenly remember where he'd seen her, then he'd grill Devin for her address. Her time in Chicago was clearly coming to an end, but where on earth would she go next? She had to find Tim. Her singular purpose had been to search for him, and now she'd have to get more aggressive about it.

CHAPTER FOURTEEN

Recent college grad, Tiara Hayes, prided herself on being too confident and secure to be intimidated by most people and situations, but her mother's next door neighbor, Tim Eckels, was not "most people." He freaked her out. He always had. She mostly kept her distance from the strange man with the coke-bottle-lensed glasses, because frankly, she found him so odd as to be disturbing. So, it was with great trepidation that she trudged from her mother's yard over to his, dreading the unknown. Marilyn had devoted her life to providing for her daughter, and for that reason alone, the beautiful blonde prepared to face the reaper. Tim had been more than persistent, for weeks, in his quest to gain employment at SubLime Sweets, and it was getting to be a bit much.

She rang the bell and waited, heart thumping,

hearing no sound coming from within the house. Tim's front porch looked like any other on the block, with decking painted to match the shutters and trim, a neatly kept stucco exterior, and a healthy fern hanging on a hook by the door. Funny, he'd never struck her as the nurturing gardener type, but the lawn and plants were healthy and precisely mani-cured. For some reason that realization gave her a chill, and she turned to trot back down the front steps, honestly relieved that he hadn't answered. She was almost to the top step when the door opened behind her.

"Hello," she heard Tim's mild, flat voice say, star-tling her.

"Oh! Uh...hi," she stammered, turning back around and walking to the door where he stood with an expectant look on his face. "I just...umm," she was suddenly at a loss for words. Tim merely blinked at her with his head tilted to one side.

She took a breath, gathering herself, and tried again. "Okay, so this is really silly and I hate to bother you, but my mom seems to think that you just aren't going to take no for an answer, when it comes to having a job at the shop, and I came over to talk to you about that," she blurted out, trying not to twist her hands nervously in front of her.

"Okay," he nodded, the expression on his face revealing nothing. "Won't you come in?" he asked, stepping back to allow her to pass.

Tiara gulped. "Uh...I...umm...come in?" she squeaked.

"Please," he nodded again, blinking at her.

Not knowing how to decline without sounding incredibly rude and suspicious, she threw caution to the winds and followed the strange man inside. If the outside of his house was quite typically Key West in style and substance, the interior was anything but, looking much like the inside of a ski lodge. The walls and ceiling were painted in a forest green color, the rooms dimly lit, and the dainty Victorian furnishings, reminiscent of those found in funeral homes, were sparse, but that was the least disturbing feature of Tim's décor. On almost every available surface rested perfectly preserved house pets. Cats, dogs, bunnies, even guinea pigs, stared into eternity with sightless eyes, making Tiara shudder as she passed through a gauntlet of them in the hallway that led to the living room.

Apparently, Tim had been in the midst of making a Coconut Cream pie when she had rung his doorbell, and he wanted to continue working on it while they chatted. He indicated a hobnailed bar stool pulled up to the breakfast bar for her to sit on, and went back to his pie preparations.

"Would you like some iced tea?" he asked, measuring some coconut milk and pouring it into a bowl.

"Umm...yeah, that'd be great, thanks," Tiara replied, weirded out by the fact that, in his own strange environment, the eerily quirky neighbor seemed almost normal. Almost. He handed her a glass of tea that actually turned out to be quite tasty, and she thanked him for it, secretly hoping that he hadn't just poisoned her.

"Do you make a lot of desserts?" she asked politely, trying to stay on his good side, and not wanting to just dive into the touchy subject of his employment, or lack thereof.

"Yes, I do. That's why your mother should have hired me," he said, without sounding bitter. "My grandmother taught me quite a bit about cooking and baking."

"You two must've been very close," she commented, sipping the cool refreshing tea, still wondering if it was going to be the death of her.

"She raised me," he responded simply, giving Tiara the impression that he'd said all that he needed to say about that subject.

"You do taxidermy?" she dared to ask, looking around.

"Clearly," he replied.

"Where did they all come from?"

He put down his mixing spoon and fixed his gaze upon her. A tiny finger of fear tickled the base of her spine as he stared for a moment before replying.

"I'm sure you have the Internet, and I'm sure you've searched for my name by now. You and your mother strike me as the type of women who would do such things," he pursed his lips briefly. "So, you surely know about the charges of animal cruelty that were brought against me years ago. Would you like to hear about the real story?" he asked mildly.

"I...uh...I'm not sure, I mean, you don't have to..." Tiara wasn't certain how to respond, wanting to hear the story, but afraid of what he might say.

He picked up his spoon again, stirring while he spoke, a faraway look in his eye.

"I was a small-town mortician. I knew every family in town because I'd seen them in their times of grief. It didn't make me a popular person, I was just the guy that everyone had to go see when the worst thing in life happened," he shrugged, focusing on his pie filling.

Tiara leaned forward in her seat, resting her elbow on the table while she took a big gulp of tea.

"More?" he asked, noting the ever-dropping level in her glass.

"Please," she nodded, chomping at the bit for him to continue.

He took his time refilling the glass, then went back to his pie making and his story.

"The town veterinarian was a boy from the city who thought he could bless our little community by imposing his will upon us poor town folk," the corner of his lip twitched downward.

"What did he try to do?" Tiara asked, engrossed in the tale already.

"He refused to euthanize pets, no matter how much they suffered. He had a deal with a vitamin supplement company that gave him kickbacks. So instead of helping them end peacefully, he stuffed pets full of useless meds and they just got sicker and sicker. Folks knew that I had access to certain chemicals that would take care of the job quite humanely, so, what the fancy doc didn't have the ethics to do, I did. The animals didn't have to suffer, and the owners didn't have to watch them suffer. Taxidermy had been a hobby of mine for years – it just seems wasteful to dispose of such beauty when an animal's soul leaves their body," he mused. "So, when owners came in and asked me to relieve their pet's suffering, I'd ask if they wanted to keep the body preserved. If they did, I did it free of charge for them, if they didn't, I asked if I could have it."

"Well...that doesn't sound so bad," Tiara was puzzled.

"It wasn't. It was a good solution for all concerned...except for the young vet who made his money trying to keep terminally ill and suffering animals alive," he grimaced, the most emotion she'd ever seen him show.

"So, the reason that the vet wouldn't euthanize the suffering pets is because he made more money by continuing to sell them all the supplements to fake treating them?" the young woman was sickened at the thought. "That's beyond disgusting."

"It's vile, pure evil. And I said so, to his face. Strangely, that made him angry," his words were weighted with sarcasm and more than a shade of contempt. "He drummed up some phony 'pet owners' who said that their animal had gone missing and that I'd stolen and killed their pets so that I could make ornaments out of them," he finished with a sigh.

"That's awful," Tiara gazed at the strange

neighbor in an entirely new light. "So, what happened? I saw that the charges were dropped."

"Yes, they were. You see, whenever I took an animal in and relieved its pain, with the owner's permission, I had them sign a form that had a registration number on it. I tattooed the number onto their pet after it had passed, and that way I had records of who had belonged to whom. Those records were what exonerated me after that veterinarian had me charged with animal cruelty. The people who had lied in court were charged with perjury and my name was cleared."

"So, everything turned out okay in the end then," Tiara commented, relieved for him.

"No, not even close. People started looking at me strangely, calling me Dr. Death behind my back. That didn't bother me much, I'd always been more comfortable around the dead than the living, but I couldn't take the funny looks. The whispers," he shook his head remembering.

The part that he couldn't tell Marilyn's young daughter was that he'd also been motivated to leave town due to the fact that his psycho wife had killed the vet in question.

"So, what did you do?" Tiara was so into his story that she'd forgotten her fear of him, mostly, and had pushed her reason for coming over to the back of her mind.

"Well, the final straw came when one of my workers was paid by the crooked veterinarian to not embalm one particular body. They already had a plan to do that periodically, and then find reasons to exhume the bodies so that I'd get "caught" and put out of business. This just happened to be one of those one in a million cases where the coroner pronounced someone deceased, verified that all bodily functions had ceased, and the person just came back."

"Like a zombie," Tiara breathed, her eyes wide.

"Except that they were fully aware and functional when that casket was opened. The family sued, and even when the boy from my office confessed to being paid off to not embalm the body, I thought it best to just leave town forever. That was the only time I'd ever had anybody come back on me, and it still gives me nightmares," he blinked behind his glasses, lost in memories. "So that's how an innocent mortician gets made out to be something that he's not...and never was," he finished, sliding his assembled pie into the oven.

"That's so awful, Mr. Eckels," the compassionate

young woman murmured. "I'm so sorry that happened to you."

"Well, I..." Tim began, when suddenly a fierce pounding rattled his front door in its frame.

He and Tiara exchanged a puzzled glance before he strode down the hall to answer it.

"Where is she?" Marilyn's voice reached her daughter's ears. "I demand that you..." she began, violating her neighbor's personal space.

"Mom! I'm right here, geez," Tiara called out, hurrying toward the door, embarrassed.

"Oh...okay, I just...." the feisty redhead trailed off, not knowing what to say.

She'd come over prepared for battle, and walked into a perfectly nice visit between neighbors.

"I've gotta go, Mr. Eckels. Thanks for talking with me," Tiara smiled and stuck out her hand.

He shook it gingerly.

"It was my pleasure," he said, having reverted back to his flat affect. "Would you like a piece of coconut pie when it's done?"

"Yeah, I'd like that," she nodded, heading for the door. "Have a good evening."

"I already have."

Tim wasn't typically one to dwell with regret on decisions that he'd made, but he was mortified that his Rhett Butler technique had backfired so spectacularly when he was trying to secure a job at the bakery. It probably seemed strange to his neighbor that a former mortician would want, so badly, to work at a beachside bakery, but the truth of it was that he wanted to keep a low profile. If the authorities were looking for him in connection with Susannah's dark acts, they'd be looking for a mortician, not a baker. He didn't think that he'd merit that kind of attention from the police, but why take a chance? The longer he could live out his life staying under the radar of law enforcement, the better.

Marilyn Hayes was successful, independent, and utterly stunning. At least if she was mad at him, it showed that she knew he was even alive.

Her daughter Tiara had an air of innocence that made Tim sad. He liked to think of himself as a bit of an innocent, and that hadn't exactly worked out well for him. He had to admit, though he didn't care to interact with other humans a great deal, Tiara's calm acceptance of what he'd had to say, had had a soothing effect on his bruised psyche. Most folks gave him strange looks and kept their distance. Tiara had listened. He wasn't accustomed to that, and if he was being honest, he had to admit that he sort of liked it.

He was clearly going to have to work on his people skills, though the thought made him shudder. Weirdos were automatically suspect. For years, he'd reveled in the solitude that being odd had provided, but now, he needed to be viewed differently. He had to blend in more, even if he hated it. And this time he'd be more careful in selecting which cinematic hero to emulate.

He needed a goal, and it wasn't difficult to select. He'd win Marilyn over, he was determined. And if he had to use Tiara to accomplish that, so be it. He hoped that he'd won an ally in the attractive young graduate, and perhaps she'd help smooth things over with her mother on his behalf. In the meantime, he'd be watching more television.

CHAPTER FIFTEEN

Susannah's legs nearly wobbled as she carefully, with as measured a pace as she could manage, walked away from the Chief of Police. The moment that she got to an exit from the alley, she took it and ran like her hair was on fire. That had been too close. She shouldn't have let Devin talk her into staying to prep. Devin. It was his fault. She kept her mind busy on the way home, thinking of inventive ways to kill the well-meaning pup, but it was merely an exercise to calm herself down. For some reason, she couldn't actually bear the thought of snuffing someone who didn't have a malicious bone in his body. Unless he became a threat to her. Or, unless he had a hidden dark side that she hadn't discovered yet.

Her hands had almost stopped shaking by the

time she slid her key into the lock of Leon's apartment, but she jumped like she'd been shot when she opened the door and her mysterious roommate stood on the other side of it.

"Cops been here," he commented, sipping at some sort of foul-smelling herbal concoction that was the color of algae.

"Oh?" Susannah managed to sound nonchalant, now achingly conscious of the killing tools that she had stashed in a backpack in the loft.

"Somebody iced a pimp a few blocks over," Leon stared at her, the pupils of his eyes indistinguishable from his espresso-colored irises. Susannah was fascinated by the phenomenon, but somehow, it chilled her.

"Did he deserve it?" she asked casually, heading to the refrigerator for some food before she passed out.

"He was a pimp," Leon shrugged, as though that explained it all.

"Dangerous line of work, I guess," Susannah feigned boredom as she pulled the ingredients for an omelet out of the fridge. "I'm making an omelet. Do you want something?" she asked.

Cooking was one of the few things that Susannah was willing to do for others. She was good at it, damn good.

"I don't eat animals," Leon raised his glass of bile in a mock salute.

"But pimps getting murdered is okay?" Susannah raised an eyebrow.

"Animals are innocent," Leon shrugged. "There's not a human on the planet who can say that. We're all motivated by self-interest. Anyway, I'm out," he turned to go. "Open the windows when you're done violating animal by-products."

Typically, such a directive, given particularly by a man, would've set Susannah's teeth on edge, but Leon was a horse of a different color. His comment hadn't been used to control her, but to lessen the impact of her presence on his own enjoyment. He was much like her in that regard.

Her omelet was done to perfection in a matter of minutes, and she took her plate up to the loft with her, to do her daily Tim searching. She'd peppered the internet with searches of Tim's name, plus mortician, mortuary, funeral, etc...and so far, had come up with exactly nothing, but she knew that he had to settle somewhere eventually. She'd also been researching strange news articles, thinking that she might find him that way. She had serious doubts as to how well he'd survive in the real world on his own, and chances were fair to middling that he'd stumble across a weird situation sooner or later.

She hadn't opened the windows yet, not wanting to freeze herself out of the apartment, but she would on her way out. Where she was going, she had no idea, but the encounter with the Chief of Police this morning birthed a restlessness within her that she couldn't ignore for much longer. She needed to think, she needed to reevaluate her plan, and she needed to find Tim.

Her obsession with finding her husband had oddly gotten worse after her encounter with Devin. As energetic and enthusiastic as the younger man had been, she still felt that there was nothing quite like Tim's quiet acquiescence to slake her thirst for the pleasures of the flesh. But there was something else too. While others viewed the introverted mortician as strange, to Susannah, his odd presence was strangely...comforting. He hadn't pried into her personal time, he'd made no demands of her, and he accepted her just as she was. Theirs hadn't been an exciting relationship, but it had been a steady one. A reliable one.

The grating sound of the buzzer at the front door resounded through the apartment, and Susannah's heart leapt in her chest. She froze, one hand holding her tablet, the other poised to strike.

"Angelica?" Devin's voice called out, making her grit her teeth.

It was as if her thoughts comparing him to Tim had conjured him. Her fingers curled in frustration, and she looked at the clock on her computer. A couple of hours had flown by without her even noticing, and as usual, she hadn't found anything of note in her search for Tim.

"Hey, Angelica...I'm worried about you. Are you okay?" Devin's voice was plaintive, which practically gave Susannah hives. She despised arrogant, dominant men like no other, but weak, sensitive ones became the objects of her scorn as well. Tim had been the only man in her life who'd seemed to know how to strike the perfect balance of 'I'm here for you,' and 'leave me the fuck alone.'

She knew that if she tried to ignore Devin, he wouldn't go away. He would just keep buzzing that horrible door bell and bleating at her with his lost sheep voice. Closing out the screen on her tablet, she picked up her empty plate, faintly disgusted by the bits of congealed egg and cheese which clung to it, and headed down the stairs.

"Angelica...?"

Another bleat from the worried lamb.

"Hold on," Susannah barked, putting her plate in the sink, running hot water on it, then opening the kitchen window.

"What?" she demanded, when she opened the door.

"Are you feeling better?" Devin asked, with a concerned smile. "You look like you feel better."

"Yeah, I'm fine," she sighed. "Just needed some food and rest."

"I'm glad that's all it was. You sure made quite an impression on the Chief of Police on your way out," he grinned.

The hairs on the back of Susannah's neck stood up.

"What?" she asked in a low voice.

"Yeah, after you left, he was asking all kinds of questions about you. What your name was, how long you'd been in the city, what neighborhood you lived in. I think it may have been because I told him what an amazing chef you are," he confided.

"What else did you tell him?" Susannah tried her best to sound casual, her fingers curling in fury.

"What little I knew," Devin shrugged. "You're kind of a mystery. Even to me," he looked down shyly. "So, are you busy right now, or...?" he looked past her hopefully.

"I'm...resting," she ran a hand through her shorn mahogany locks. "Even though I feel much better, I'm still kind of woozy from this morning, you know?"

She was glad that the excuse of illness allowed her to get away with not even trying to smile. She was seething. The Chief had asked questions, and Devin had answered them. She'd like to kill them both, but that wasn't a terribly wise choice at the moment.

"Oh, sure," he nodded. "I just thought...I don't know...that you might want some company or something," he blushed, even the tips of his ears turning pink.

"Nah, I'm too tired to be good company."

She *was* tired. Tired of her plans being screwed up by odd encounters.

"We could watch TV or a movie or something," he tried again, still either unwilling or unable to take no for an answer.

Netflix and chill? Really? Susannah mentally rolled her eyes.

"I'm just gonna crash out for a bit, but I'll see you tomorrow," she lied.

By tomorrow she might be gone, and even if she wasn't, she wouldn't be seeing Devin. He was trying to get close to her, like a mouse accidentally entreating a cobra to be its friend. He had no idea who or what she was, and it had to stay that way, which meant she had to ghost him. Working at the Co-op for food and doing her own thing had been easy and convenient, but it was clearly time to move on. She just wished that she had some indication of where Tim might be starting his new life, apart from her.

"Oh, good," the poor lad lit up like a Christmas tree. It was sickening.

He took a step forward and awkwardly leaned toward her, like he wanted to give her a kiss, but was afraid of rejection. It was a valid fear. Susannah stepped back, out of lip-lock range.

"Talk to you later," she said quickly, and shut the door.

"Okay, bye," was the muffled response from the other side.

CHAPTER SIXTEEN

While Timothy Eckels still hadn't gained the trust of his attractive neighbor, Marilyn, nor secured a job, he had at least managed to form a casually pleasant relationship with her daughter, Tiara, who would stop and chat a bit if she saw him outside. He dropped into the pie shop every now and again, if he happened to experience a craving during his daily walks on the beach, and hadn't yet been thrown out or turned away, though he remained tongue-tied and awkward when he encountered Marilyn.

Tim's time in Florida had burnished his white skin to a faint tan, and exposure to sunlight and salt air had combined to give his mouse-brown hair golden highlights. He still wasn't a terribly attractive man by any means, but the sun-kissed glow at least made his appearance slightly less cadaverous. He

and his cat, Maisie, had carved out a mellow existence in their quiet cul-de-sac, and with the exception of some unnerving calls where no one spoke,
his life was fairly normal. As normal as the husband
of a fugitive serial killer could hope to be, at any rate.

The former mortician had no illusions about his
charm and grace, or lack thereof. He'd always been
an outsider, and was more than okay with that. What
he didn't realize is that sometimes other people
found his quiet, contemplative demeanor to be...
creepy. His eyes bulging behind coke-bottle thick
glasses looked buggy and a bit leering, and his habit
of staring into space while puzzling through social
interactions could be off-putting. It also simply
didn't occur to him that when he structured his
walks on the beach to coincide with Marilyn and
Tiara's beach yoga class, that it might unnerve them
to see him watching, transfixed, from beneath a
stand of palms near the boardwalk.

As he settled into position beneath the trees,
water bottle in hand, to observe the class on this
particular morning, he noted that Marilyn was not
in attendance. She and Tiara usually staked out
their spots in the middle of the second row. They
faced the ocean, which meant that Tim saw the class
from behind, but their graceful, fluid movements

soothed him somehow, despite the fact that their supremely fit male teacher seemed to be a bit of an arrogant peacock.

Tim wondered where Marilyn might be, and hoped that she was well. He'd have to peer through the hedge between their houses to see if she was taking in the sun on her back patio, as she usually did when she wasn't feeling well. He didn't have much of a life of his own, so the restless mortician contented himself with keeping tabs on his neighbors. They fascinated him.

"Nice view, huh?" a masculine voice to his left startled Tim from his reverie.

Not quite certain what the muscle-bound young man meant, he nodded cautiously.

"I like the ocean," he said simply, dropping his gaze back to the yoga class.

"The ocean," the man snickered. "Yeah, that's what I'm checking out too, dude."

"What are you implying?" Tim frowned, blinking up at the young man.

"Don't get your boxers in a bunch, man."

All traces of mirth left the man's face and he looked menacing, towering above the mortician. When Tim ignored him, he spoke again.

"I wonder how those ladies would feel, knowing

that you're sitting up here checking them out in their tight little yoga clothes," he threatened.

"You're filthy," Tim muttered, standing up and brushing the sand from the back of his walking shorts.

"Takes one to know one," the guy smirked, dodging in front of Tim to impede his progress.

"Move aside," Tim said calmly.

He'd dealt with bullies his entire life. This one was no different, but there was something in his eyes when he gazed at the exercising women that Tim didn't care for at all. He knew that look. He'd seen it in his wife's eyes on occasion...when she came back from engaging in her...hobby. Hunger. Need. That look never led to anything good.

"Tough guy, huh?" the insufferable young man mocked him. "What if I don't move? What are you going to do about it, wuss?" he taunted.

Wuss. Tim had been called worse.

"Don't make me do this," he sighed, not looking at his tormentor, but keeping his eyes on the sand at his feet.

"Oh, I'm so scared," the guy let out a high pitched laugh that made the hair on the back of Tim's neck stand on end.

He had no choice now. Some bullies had to learn

the hard way. Tim had been pushed around quite a bit in his life, and usually he just let the bullies have their fun until they became tired of getting no reaction, then he'd go on his way. Sometimes, they needed a lesson in humility.

"It didn't have to come to this," Tim muttered, right before he made a fist with his left hand and punched the punk right in his tender parts.

When the guy let out a whoof of surprise and bent double, his hands going to his crotch, Tim locked his hands together and brought them down with a thunk on the back of the thickly muscled neck of the miscreant. He went down with a thump, and lay writhing under the tree. Tim stepped nimbly out of reach of one scrabbling hand, and hopped up onto the boardwalk. He wasn't going home. He'd seen the look in the bully's eyes, and he was going to be nearby, making sure that Tiara got home, unscathed.

He knew the path that she took home. One of the things that he respected about her was the fact that she had a pattern to her life, a routine that rarely varied, and while Tim could see the appeal of that, it didn't necessarily make for a safe existence. The irony of that was that, while he could see the flaw in Tiara choosing to live that way, he had no thought of applying that same wisdom to his own life. He had a routine. If anyone happened to be watching...it might not be the best thing for his safety.

Tim stationed himself a few blocks away, near the side of a building, where he wouldn't be observed. He knew that Tiara would pass by him on her way home, and he wanted to make certain that the thug from the beach wasn't following her. Much to his surprise, the cocky yoga instructor accompanied Tiara on her trek home, with Tim slipping between houses and yards to keep tabs on them. As unpleasant as the tanned instructor, who was far too old for Tiara, in Tim's biased opinion, seemed, he was a much more benign alternative to the bully.

When they reached Marilyn's house, the two of them stood talking and laughing for a few minutes. Tim was close enough to see them, but unable to hear their conversation, and hoped that he wouldn't soon be witnessing something so nause-ating as a goodbye kiss. His heart sank as he assumed that Tiara would welcome such an advance, but it didn't appear that the overconfident yoga instructor had picked up on that particular signal. Tim was no expert in romance, to be sure, but he'd observed human behavior for long enough to know a good flirtation when he saw one. It made him doubly glad not to be on the receiving end of it. Romance meant entanglement, and with entanglement came issues, sometimes murderous issues. He sighed and glanced at his watch, waiting for Tiara to go inside, so that he could get home to his cat.

Dismayed that she was all dressed up and walking alone at night, Tim had followed Tiara to a house that was on the razor's edge of a bad neighborhood, where a raging party shook the interior walls. From his spot between bushes in the side yard, he kept an eye on his young neighbor. So far, she was safe, but he had a really bad feeling about this event. He'd been there for about ten minutes when he heard stumbling footsteps heading in his direction.

A young man staggered into the bushes, clearly in the throes of alcohol poisoning and Tim darted back just in time to avoid having his shoes spattered with used beer and onion dip. The stench that arose from the primitive act was foul and profound, even for a man who worked with the dead. The young man berated him in between heaves.

"Creeper, quit watching me," he bellowed, bending double to hurl again.

"Get outta here," he ordered, lurching toward Tim, holding on to the bushes for balance.

He might be sloppy drunk, but he was also large, loud and belligerent, so the meek mortician jogged out of the yard and toward home before the vomitous lout drew too much undue attention. He'd simply have to hope that Tiara exercised a measure of good sense while she was at the party, and he'd wait up to make certain that she arrived home unscathed.

Sitting in the dark, on his front porch, with Maisie sleeping contentedly in his lap, Tim waited... and waited. The hour grew later and later, and he didn't feel even the least bit sleepy. Every nerve ending jangled with even the softest of sounds as he watched for Tiara. It was no mystery why he was so concerned about her. She treated him like a human being. She talked to him and listened when he answered. She was also young enough that there was no possibility of a relationship, so they could both be themselves without worrying about making an impression. She was his friend. At the moment, his only friend.

Tim heard them coming well before he saw them. Tires squealed, turning the corner into the neighborhood, and music blared from behind the closed windows of a rusty-laden clunker. The car was driving much too fast, and lurched to the curb abruptly, squeaking the tires again. Tiara opened the passenger door and got out, stumbling a bit and passing a hand over her eyes in confusion. Expecting to see the yoga instructor emerge from the driver's side, Tim was appalled to see the muscle-bound punk who had been leering at the yoga class on the beach.

Tiara leaned against the car, looking dazed, and the bully came around to her side of the car, putting a tree trunk arm on either side of her, blocking her exit. She shook her head several times during the course of the conversation, and when the punk moved in close to kiss her, she turned her head to the side and vomited, splashing him, the car and herself. The bully didn't react well, jumping back with an expletive and shoving her aside so abruptly that she lost her balance and fell to the ground, where she lay sobbing weakly. Stripping off his sodden shirt, the bully wiped himself down as best he could, then, throwing the shirt at Tiara, he got back into the car and tore away from the curb. Rather than getting up, Tiara laid her head down on the fine, soft grass of the lawn.

When Tim sprinted to her side, Tiara was unconscious. Grabbing her phone from the back pocket of her once-white linen shorts, he scrolled through her contacts until he found the one that he was looking for. Mom. Without hesitation, he tapped the number to make the call.

"Hey honey, I'm at the movie, is everything..." Marilyn's voice on the other end was cheery, but Tim had no choice, he had to interrupt.

"Ms. Hayes, this is Timothy Eckels, your neighbor. Your daughter seems to be very ill and was just deposited on your front lawn by a young man who didn't have the best of intentions. Would you like me to call an ambulance?" Tim asked, with no trace of awkwardness.

It's funny how emergencies can clarify one's focus.

"Oh, no, is she breathing? Is she okay?" Marilyn demanded. *"What happened to her? I swear I will kill..."* she began to rant.

"I'm going to call the ambulance now. She's breathing, but her pupils are dilated like she's been drugged," Tim replied, reluctant to waste any more time.

"Oh god. Yes, call them. I'm on my way, I'll be there in about ten minutes." Click.

Marilyn screeched into her driveway mere minutes after the ambulance arrived. By the time she'd hurried over, the EMTs were loading her precious daughter onto a gurney and wheeling her into the ambulance. As she stepped up into the back to ride with Tiara, she glanced at Tim.

"Thank you for calling an ambulance," she said, her eyes flashing fire. "But you had better believe that once I get home, you and I are going to have a little chat," she growled. "And if I find out that you had anything to do with this..." she threatened.

"Sorry, ma'am, we need to close the doors for transport," one of the EMTs interrupted.

Tim raised a hand in farewell and watched as the ambulance rushed toward the hospital, sirens silent, but lights flashing.

CHAPTER SEVENTEEN

Susannah had a plan. The realtor with whom Tim had listed their former marital cottage was a busy lady. She had been a stone fortress of discretion when Susannah had tried to secure information as to Tim's whereabouts, but that just meant that the killer had to be a bit more clever. She made sure when she called this time that the powerhouse realtor was out of the office, hosting an open house that had been advertised in the local paper. Her hope was that she'd be able to outsmart the assistant who would be inevitably answering the phone at the real estate office while the realtor was otherwise occupied. Since her time in Chicago was coming to a close, Susannah's fixation on finding her husband, Tim, had morphed into an obsession. She would stop at nothing to find her mate. What she'd do with him when she did was still very much up in the air.

"Hello," she said sweetly, when the realtor's assistant answered the phone. "My name is Francine Biggels. Your client, Timothy Eckels, did my late husband George's funeral before he left town, and I need to pay off the balance of my account. He told me to just forget about it, but I'm a woman who pays my bills, you know? Anyway, so I was hoping that maybe you good folks had a mailing address for Mr. Eckels," she rambled, channeling the babbling secretary that she remembered from her high school.

There was an agonizing silence as the young assistant hesitated.

"Well, we're really not supposed to give out that kind of information," she said ruefully.

"Really? Oh, dear, that's such a pity," Susannah gave her voice a disappointed lilt. "I just figured... with that awful thing that happened, the poor dear could probably use the money," she lowered her voice to a conspiratorial whisper.

Another hesitation. Susannah held her breath.

"He probably could use the money, poor guy. And all we have for him is a Post Office box address anyway..." the assistant wavered.

Susannah clenched her hand so hard that her nails embedded themselves in her palm, and the pain helped her to focus so that she didn't blurt out something stupid. She quite literally bit her tongue to keep from scaring off the assistant by begging. She stayed silent, allowing the dense young woman to deliberate as long as she needed to. Just as she was about to open her mouth and thank her for her time, the assistant spoke again.

"Okay, I probably shouldn't do this, but I can give you his P.O. box. I don't see what that could possibly hurt, right?"

Susannah's heart thudded in her chest and she had to swallow the bile that rose in the back of her throat. She was about to find her Tim. Well, not find him exactly, but at least find the town that he lived in. She was so close that she could taste it.

"Oh, that would be so sweet of you!" she cooed. "It's just been weighing on my conscience that I haven't paid him yet. He did such a good job with my George. He looked like he was just taking a nap."

At least that statement reflected a touch of reality. Tim was an absolute artist when it came to preparing the dead. Susannah had always respected that about him. Her hand trembled with a strange longing as she wrote down the address that the assistant gave her. There he was. Her Timmy. She'd found him. In Key West, Florida.

She tried to keep her voice steady as she thanked the clueless receptionist, then put her head back against the sofa and just shook. Closing her eyes, an unfamiliar sensation bubbled up within her chest and she began to laugh...long, and loud, and gleefully. Susannah laughed until tears filled her eyes. When the fierce utterance, which was only a mockery of mirth, had subsided, she was left with a predatory grin spreading slowly over her face.

"I'm coming for you, Timmy," she whispered, a white-hot thrill shooting through her core. "I'm coming."

Susannah loved the fact that the artsy types who inhabited her building held great belief in the honor system. She cleaned out the cookie jar where Leon hoarded his cash, finding nearly seven hundred dollars, then she systematically went door to door in the building. If the occupant answered the door, she asked to borrow twenty dollars. In every case but one, she got it, even if it sometimes came in the form of bills, coins and coupons for free coffee. The one who didn't have twenty to give her gave her ten instead and told her there'd be more after his shift at the bar tonight. If the occupant wasn't home, she tried the handle and slipped silently inside those that had been left unlocked, ferreting out any cash she could find. All in all, by the time she left the ramshackle building in Old Town that had been her home for the past few weeks, she was nearly three thousand dollars richer. That was plenty of money to get her to Florida, and she hadn't even had to touch any filthy homeless people. Yet.

"Hey, Angelica!" Devin greeted her with nothing short of delight when she entered the kitchen through the back door.

He was peeling potatoes over a piece of parchment paper, which he'd run through the composting machine later.

"Oh, Angie, I am so glad to see you," Shiloh turned from her cutting board at the center island. "Can you please take over for me here? I thought I could hold out for a while longer, but if I don't feed this baby soon," she referred to the infant strapped to the front of her, "my breasts are just going to explode, and nobody wants to see that."

Shiloh untied her apron and handed it to Susannah, who took it, then went and set her bulging backpack in the pantry. She hadn't intended to help with lunch, but a good meal before hitting the road certainly couldn't hurt. As long as the police chief didn't decide to drop by again. She had a reason for being here – lunch was just a bonus.

"So, your backpack looks really full," Devin observed, once Shiloh left the room.

Susannah could tell by the look on his face that he'd figured out what was happening and was bracing himself for the news. She conjured up her best impression of someone who was sad but determined.

"Yeah," she said softly, nodding. "I heard about a job opportunity out in California, and I'd be crazy to turn it down," she lied, hoping he'd remember the details when the police inevitably asked him where she was.

"Wow, that's a long way from Chicago," Devin tried to smile and failed. "I'm happy for you, though. Is it a chef position?"

"Yep, I'll be working at a fine dining restaurant on the beach in Del Mar," Susannah picked up Shiloh's knife and began slicing vegetables. "What are we making here?" she asked, surveying the selection of items on the island.

"Pulled pork with slaw and beans. The pickles

are homemade," Devin's voice was morose. "Should I come with you?" he asked, seeming scared of her potential reaction.

"To California?" Susannah's brows shot skyward.

She hadn't anticipated this.

"Yeah," he shrugged, adding brown sugar to what would become the barbecue sauce for the pork.

He didn't look at her, which was fortunate. Her mouth had dropped open in surprise and she closed it quickly, before he could notice and be offended. He was an innocent. She didn't want to hurt him any more than she had to.

"You can't do that, Devin," she tried her best to sound sad. "You have a life here. There are people who depend on you. I'm just passing through. That's all I was ever doing here, really. Chicago was a stepping stone for me, but you have a chance to carve out a niche for yourself. I can't take that away from you, and you shouldn't take it away from yourself," she urged him, trying to remember how her mother used to dispense faux-motherly advice on the rare occasion that she was motivated to try.

"Yeah, I guess that makes sense," he moped, stirring the barbecue sauce. "So, this is it? When are you leaving?"

"Right after lunch."

"Does Leon know?" he asked.

Susannah shook her head.

"No, I just got the email from the restaurant this morning. He was already gone."

"Do you have to go, like, right now? I mean, it seems kind of fast. Maybe you could go tomorrow or next week or something and we could at least have a goodbye dinner..." he trailed off.

Susannah knew what he really wanted before she left, and it wasn't dinner.

"I'd really like that," she lied, her voice syrupy-sweet. "But they want me to start right away."

Devin frowned, chopping onions like his life depended on it.

"Well, do you need a ride to the airport or anything?"

Susannah stared at him.

"Devin, you don't have a car."

"Yeah, I know," he looked down and sighed. "But maybe we could share an Uber or something...I don't know," he shrugged.

"That's really sweet of you," Susannah nodded. "But I think it'll be much less painful for both of us if we say goodbye here and leave it at that."

"Sure, I get it," Devin agreed, sounding like he

didn't get it, at all. "Can I at least kiss you goodbye?" he asked quietly, glancing about to make sure he wasn't overheard.

"Of course."

They worked in silence for a while, Susannah trying to come up with scenarios that would let her out of the long, sad goodbye that Devin was obviously counting on. Lunch was tasty, even if she would have preferred brioche to the wheat buns that were used, and when Devin couldn't finish his, she finished it for him. She almost felt sorry for him, but was a bit disgusted by his emotional response. She'd given the lad no reason to like her as much as he thought he did. He didn't even know her. If he'd gotten to know her, he would've been utterly horrified, and she would've been forced to kill him. And she wouldn't have regretted it in the least.

Her thoughts were only of one man. The only man who'd ever shared her body, her space, and perhaps the one shred of her heart that wasn't withered and cold, awaited her in Florida. She'd never been to the beach, and was quite sure she'd hate it, but if that's where her Timmy was...off she would go.

After a clumsy kiss, where Devin tried his best to shove his tongue down her throat, while groping her one last time and trying his level best not to cry,

Susannah slipped through the alley and away from the co-op. Her backpack was laden with some choice knives that she'd managed to pilfer when Devin had taken a bathroom break. He'd tasted minty fresh when he kissed her, so she figured he'd brushed his teeth in honor of their last kiss. Sweet kid. Dumb, but sweet.

CHAPTER EIGHTEEN

Susannah both loved and hated being on the road. While it would be nice to head south, now that the omnipresent winds of Chicago were growing chillier by the day, there had been a certain comfort to being an anonymous face among millions. Now, her anonymity had been compromised. The police chief had asked questions. It was time to move on. With any luck, if they had indeed figured out who she was, they'd go back to Devin, ask questions, and move their search to California. The thought made her smile. She enjoyed being the cause of a wild goose chase.

She'd taken the train to where she'd left Angelica's car under the L and was astonished to see that the old rust-bucket was still there. Apparently. it was such a beater that even the tow yards didn't want it.

Wiping a coating of grime from the driver's side window so that she could peer inside, she saw a lump on the backseat that looked undeniably human.

"Great," she muttered, not relishing the impending encounter with the homeless person who had taken up residence in the vehicle.

She did a mental calculation as to how to best approach the situation. She knew she'd be faster, stronger and smarter than whoever was sleeping in the car, so she wouldn't have to actually kill them. Cleaning blood out of the backseat in broad daylight would be such a pain. She didn't have the time or the desire to mess with that.

The squatter would undoubtedly have belongings in the car, which would smell awful, but she could get rid of the person now, and clean out the car later. Actually, if she ever had to dump the car, the DNA found in it would belong to the homeless person who had occupied the backseat, rather than her, which would be a good thing. There had to be hair, skin and sweat DNA galore floating around in there now. Silver linings could come from the oddest of sources sometimes.

Noting that the car was locked, Susannah put one gloved hand on the handle of the back door and turned the key twice in the lock of the driver's door, unlocking the entire car. The lump inside didn't budge. Flinging the back door open in order to startle the occupant, she reached inside, wondering which end of the human she was about to grab, and took hold of the pile of blankets, trash and newspapers, under which, someone was currently thrashing about. Latching onto what were obviously shoe-clad feet beneath the mess, Susannah gave a mighty yank, and backpedaled, pulling the person out of the car, not caring when their head clonked on the floorboard on its way out.

There was a muffled exclamation of surprise, as the vagrant thrashed about, trying to emerge from the tangle of possessions.

"Hey!" a young man, maybe in his early twenties, filthy and thin, uncovered his head and rolled out of the blankets and coats under which he'd slept, indignant.

"Sorry," Susannah shrugged. "My car."

She slammed the back door shut, after pulling a few of the larger items of clothing and sleeping gear out of the backseat and throwing it on the unfortunate youth, who sat on the ground, staring at her, dumbfounded.

"That was my house," the kid protested weakly.

"Then you need to reevaluate your life choices," Susannah remarked, slamming the driver's door behind her and locking herself in.

The stale stench of a plethora of body odors and unhealthy food and drink assaulted her nostrils, so she opened the windows, letting icy air pour into the car, cleansing it.

Her plan was simple. She'd make her way to Florida as fast as humanly possible, keeping to backroads whenever possible and fortifying herself with copious amounts of caffeine. Right now, adrenaline hummed through her veins like a thousand live wires, but that would only carry her just so far. Sleep was unthinkable at this point. Susannah had a focus. Timmy.

It was real. She knew where he was, relatively speaking, and she was on her way to him. She never stopped to think about what she might encounter when she arrived. Timothy Eckels might appear to be meek and mild, but he had a streak in him that had made the other kids shy away when he was growing up. He was different. Odd to be sure. But it was more than that. Perhaps what had snapped within him at the death of his beloved grandmother had merely served to unleash a deliberate sort of darkness that filled his soul at times. A fatal strength.

It wasn't that Tim wasn't fundamentally good. He cared passionately about animals, and had a rather benign disinterest in humanity, but the underlying characteristic which had guided him from the time that he was small, weak, and picked upon, was his profound insistence upon justice. Innocents shouldn't be hurt, and the guilty deserved to be punished. An eye for an eye was a concept with which the mortician wholeheartedly agreed...and he'd found himself married to a serial killer.

Susannah had no idea what her quiet, unassuming husband was capable of. He'd been underestimated his entire nerdy life.

Stopping at a busy toll road oasis just outside of Chicago, she rolled up the rest of the vagrant's belongings and stuffed them into an outdoor trash can. It felt very much like it had been a hundred years since her last meal with Devin, so she went inside the minimart, planning to buy a water and a piece of fruit to tide her over until she decided to stop for an on-the-go dinner. Grabbing an apple and a ridiculously overpriced bottle of water, she stood impatiently in line. Everything about her life was in fast-forward right now, and queueing up behind her bovine-like fellow humans as they milled about, slowly going through the motions of life, was maddening. She gritted her teeth as the clerk, who seemed to be moving through molasses, processed transaction after transaction. The man in front of her ordered lottery tickets, all with self-selected numbers, which made them take even longer to process. Susannah kept her fury at bay by picturing what it would be like to peel his skin away with a very sharp paring knife.

Simmering, she glanced at the tiny television that the clerk had behind the counter, and nearly passed out when she saw her own face on the screen. It was an old picture, from before she'd been apprehended, so she still had long blond hair, and carried roughly twenty extra pounds, but she imagined that she still looked much the same. Swallowing convulsively, her eyes darting about, she froze. She had to act normal, so as not to draw undue attention to herself, but she wondered if anyone had noticed.

The lottery guy finally finished, and her image on the television stayed at the bottom of the screen, with a tagline that said, 'possibly armed and dangerous,' while the reporter spoke with the hayseed sheriff that Susannah had managed to elude.

"You wanna sack?" the clerk who had rung up her snack asked, turning toward the television to grab a bag.

"Nope, I'm fine, thanks," Susannah blurted, grabbing her items.

Behind her in line stood a single mother, holding the hand of a grubby, pot-bellied, six year old girl. When Susannah turned to leave, the little girl, who had been staring at the television, stared at her in big-eyed wonder. She tugged on her mother's sleeve and pointed at the television. Susannah fled.

"Hey, you forgot your change," the cud-chewing clerk observed, calling after her.

"Keep it," Susannah directed, ducking out the door.

Flinging herself into the car, she turned the engine over and was about to back out of her parking space when there was a knock on her window. Heart in her throat, she glanced up quick and saw a police officer peering in at her. Head pounding with rage and adrenaline, Susannah squeezed her eyes shut for a moment, squelching the murderous impulses that rose up within her. What should she do? Back out with screaming tires and make a run for it? Chances are, she wouldn't get far. Locking eyes with the stern-faced officer, she decided to engage him and see how much he knew.

She'd come too far. She knew where her Timmy was, and no beat-walking cop was going to stand between her and Florida. She'd kill if she had to. She rolled down the window, blazing anger swimming behind what she hoped was a casual smile.

"Hello," her face felt stiff, and her thigh muscles were rigid.

"Where ya headed?" the officer asked, his eyes boring into hers.

"Home," she shrugged, hating the tremor in her voice.

He stared at her for a moment.

"You might not make it," he said quietly.

The color drained from Susannah's face. Her stomach flipped over, leaving her feeling as though she might vomit, and an eerie, focused calm came over her as she weighed different options for ending the officer's life.

"Ma'am?" he said, snapping her out of her murderous thoughts.

"Huh?" she gaped at him, her desire to kill flitting in her stomach and making her twitch.

"I said, you need to put air in your back tire on the passenger side. It's low. The air is over there, around the side of the building. Do you need any help with it?" he asked.

Apparently, he was merely low key, rather than sinister. Susannah wanted nothing more than to get out of there as soon as possible. The child who had been behind her in line came out of the mini-mart with her mother, and Susannah shifted to the side a bit so that the kid's line of sight was obscured by the thick body of the cop. She couldn't risk letting him go into the mini-mart where he might see her on the clerk's TV, so she forced a smile.

"Oh, yes, please," she nodded, affecting what she hoped was a helpless and relieved air that disgusted her to no end.

She'd grown up on a farm and had learned to slaughter and butcher animals, run power tools, cook gourmet meals, and maintain a side business selling bizarre art pieces, that she'd created, before she was even out of junior high. She could change the damn tire if she wanted to, along with the oil and transmission fluid, but she needed to keep the officer occupied, so she played the sickening part of damsel in distress.

Driving carefully to the air station, she got out of the car and stood by the officer while he put air in her tire, pretending to listen attentively as he explained how the gauge worked and why proper air pressure was so important. The little girl who had been in the store stared at Susannah as her mother drove past, and if looks could kill, the poor tot would've been slain on the spot.

The killer's heart rate didn't return to normal until she was several miles down the road. The game had changed. Her face was appearing on national news now, which only added to her sense of urgency. She had to get to Tim, before the authorities closed in on her.

Susannah Eckels couldn't care less about palm trees and sunshine, but she had to admit that the warmer temperatures made sleeping in the car much more pleasant. She'd made it to southern Georgia before she finally gave in to the fact that her body needed sleep in order to function properly. She was jittery from having consumed copious amounts of caffeine, but her overwhelming fatigue compelled her to pull off the road. She'd chosen a neighborhood of dubious reputation in which to park, knowing that no one in the shabby homes around her would bother to call the police because a rusty car had parked there overnight. She had rolled up her windows, locked the doors and dared anyone to disturb her. She slept for three hours and woke just before dawn, feeling reinvigorated.

Susannah had been too worried about being seen to stop for a dinner meal, so she woke up ravenous and dehydrated, her mouth feeling fuzzy and dry. After filling up Angelica's rusty little car with gas and going through a drive-through for a breakfast sandwich, four cartons of orange juice and a yogurt parfait, all of which she consumed in an obscure corner of the parking lot, she was on her way once more. She was close. She could feel it. Though South Georgia was a full day's drive from Key West, she knew that she'd be there by dinner-time. The thought that she could potentially find her husband in the next twenty-four hours drove her with a single-minded determination.

He was a day away. She trembled. She thought of the knives in her backpack and she wondered. Time would tell.

CHAPTER NINETEEN

"It would seem that I have some apologizing to do," Marilyn Hayes confessed, fidgeting nervously on Tim's front porch.

Tim stood, leaning against his doorjamb, unconsciously wiping his hands on the apron he wore. He'd been preparing to preserve a dead robin that he'd found, and was quite certain that that little tidbit of information would send his rather judgmental neighbor scurrying back to the safety of her own home. Her daughter would have understood, but Marilyn...not so much.

"Oh?" he asked, pushing heavy glasses up on the bridge of his nose with the back of his wrist.

"The doctors determined that Tiara had been given a date rape drug at the party that she went to last night. She suspected that the guy who gave her a ride home was the one who did it, because he was pressuring her to invite him in. She doesn't remember much, but she does remember seeing you watching from the porch when that guy was..." Marilyn clamped her lips shut and shook her head, shuddering. "Anyway, who knows what might have happened to her if you hadn't gotten her some help as quickly as you did," Marilyn's eyes clouded with tears. "So, I'm sorry, and thank you," she looked away, swiping at her eyes.

"What is his name?" Tim's tone was ominous.

Marilyn's head snapped up, and when she saw the look in his eyes, it seemed that she liked it.

"I don't know, but I'll find out. Apparently, he's friends with our beach yoga instructor," there was a sinister gleam in Marilyn's eyes.

"And does the yoga instructor know of this incident?" Tim asked.

"I don't think so," Marilyn shook her head.

"Don't tell him. See if you can find out without telling him why," the former mortician instructed, an idea brewing.

"What are you going to do?" Marilyn whispered.

"Nothing at all," Tim lied, anger burning in the

pit of his stomach. "Maybe talk to him about being a gentleman."

"Like that will help," Marilyn rolled her eyes. "Anyway, you've been more than helpful. I'm sorry I was rude to you," she turned to go.

"Ms. Hayes," the steel in Tim's mellow voice stopped her in her tracks.

She turned, raising her eyebrows in an unspoken question.

"I'll want that name when you get it. And any other information you can find."

The look on his bland face sent shivers up Marilyn's spine, despite the cloying heat of the Florida morning.

"Okay," she nodded, turning for home.

Nobody messes with Marilyn Hayes' daughter. Nobody.

Tiara confided in Marilyn that the house she'd gone to for the party was being rented by their yoga instructor, the punk who'd drugged her, and another guy who worked in a restaurant. She only knew the punk by his first name, Conor, and thought that he might work at a gym. Marilyn relayed the information to Tim, not knowing why he wanted it, and not caring what he might do with it. If revenge could be exacted upon the putrid predator, and neither she nor Tiara had to be involved, so much the better. Karma can be a bitch.

Tiara's yoga instructor's schedule hadn't been hard to find. His business was advertised online, and frankly, Tim was appalled at the prices that he charged for his classes. As for the third roommate, it was easy to deduce what hours someone who worked at a restaurant might be gone, and after watching the party house from a distance, because his hiding spot in the bushes had been fouled, he was able to pinpoint when each of the three men who rented the small house came and went. The target of his ire would be alone in the house from roughly six to nine o'clock every evening. The restaurant worker took the dinner shift, and the yoga instructor led a meditation group at the local library. Those events were even more expensive than the yoga, which made Tim roll his eyes.

To say that Conor the gym rat was a creature of

habit was a profound understatement. He did exactly the same things at exactly the same time, in exactly the same way, every day. It seemed that the only variety in his routine came on weekend nights, when he socialized with his roommates. That sort of regularity would make Tim's task much easier. The lunk came home from the gym every day around seven o'clock in the evening, downed two bottles of a blue-colored sports drink, and played video games for a couple of hours. His restaurant working roommate left before he got home, usually around five o'clock, and the yogi went on his way at six and would be gone until nine.

Tim waited in the shadows of a neighbor's yard until the yoga instructor left for the evening, then slipped through two backyards to enter the rental home through the unlocked back door. Earlier in the day, he'd astonished a young street tough by requesting to buy a rather large quantity of a drug that would knock Conor out quickly and render him unable to function for at least a few hours. Revenge, coupled with irony, was quite the heady combination.

"You too weird to be a cop," the small-time dealer had said, sizing Tim up.

"Correct. And my money is just as good as anyone else's," had been Tim's mild reply.

He'd gone on his way, bag of drugs in hand, the drug dealer staring after him, shaking his head and counting his money.

Tim had thought out the details ahead of time, and had made certain to reglue the safety rings around the caps of the blue sports drinks after loading them with heavy doses of the drug that was quite possibly of the same variety as the one that had been slipped into Tiara's drink. Once his work was done, he left the house and stationed himself in the bushes to await Conor's arrival.

It shouldn't take long for the drugs to kick in, due to the sheer amount that Tim had used, combined with the fact that Conor slammed his post workout drinks down in seconds. Once the substance hit his system, he'd be out like a light. Tim hadn't considered that there might be a foul taste after the drug was combined with the blue liquid, but he hoped that it would be consumed quickly enough so as not to matter. His car was parked a few blocks away, and once the bodybuilder was down for the count, he'd simply pull it into the alley behind the house, under trees that would conceal his actions, and load the unfortunate young would-be rapist into the backseat.

The former mortician watched with a degree of satisfaction that bordered upon glee as Conor followed his normal routine to the letter. He'd had his drink, and within a matter of minutes after sitting down to play video games, he swayed a bit, then collapsed, face first onto the coffee table. Tim jogged to his car and parked it in the alley, going in the perpetually unlocked back door.

Conor was heavier than Tim had anticipated, and he knew there'd be abrasions on the young man's backside from being dragged across the house. Fortunately, he hadn't bled when his face hit the coffee table, so there was no mess to clean up. Dragging his bulk across the scrabbly patch of lawn in the backyard was far more challenging than hauling him around inside the house had been, and by the time Tim drove away after maneuvering the large man into his backseat, he was red-faced and sweating from the exertion.

In an odd sort of way, it felt really good to be back in the saddle again, and Tim hummed as he went about his work, alternating his methods only slightly. As strange as it might seem to most of the population, the former mortician had always enjoyed his work. The dead were far more amiable than the living, as it turned out.

He used a hairdryer to dry out the lips so that they could be glued. The eyes were a bit trickier, jelly-filled things that they were. He had no dome caps to set on them, rounding out the contours to perfection, so he had to settle for an overall profile that was less than ideal, but made it work none-theless. He thought about actually stitching the insides of the fingers together, rather than simply gluing them, but it was far messier and much more time consuming, so he elected to sacrifice the stitching in favor of a more expedient solution, and uncapped his glue once more.

Brushing the hair to a sheen, he applied hair-spray to keep it perfectly in place, then set about putting on makeup. Usually for a gentleman, he'd apply a natural-looking overall tint, sculpt some planes and shadows after the fact, and top it off with the slightest tinge of rouge, for an ironically healthful glow. Tim loved irony, particularly when the carriers of it were the somnolent faces of the dead. This one, however was special, and got the full treatment, complete with bright blue eyeshadow and lipstick, a mockery of his unwarranted machismo. He had to chuckle to himself when he surveyed the final masterpiece.

"Who's the beauty now?" he practically giggled with glee.

Shouldering the heavy mound of flesh, taking particular care not to disturb his aesthetic work, he dumped the unfortunate sap once more into the backseat of his car and headed for the docks. The night was warm, but a lovely breeze wafted in through the open windows, and Tim was content. Arriving at his destination, he found two large, tough-looking young men who seemed to be of questionable character, and had a conversation with them, entirely unaware that his every move was being watched. A large sum of money transferred from the former mortician to the meaty palms of the misguided youths, and they came over to claim his prize from the backseat. Taking care to vacuum the backseat with a mini-vac, which he then emptied into the water, he completed his goal, and turned toward home, whistling a happy tune.

A figure emerged from the shadows when Tim was out of sight, and boldly approached the two young toughs who were in the process of taking out their rage upon the motionless bundle that Tim had left with them. The somewhat paunchy former mortician had taken video of the man in the makeup before he left, chuckling to himself in a manner that even creeped out the hired thugs. This new arrival puzzled them even more than the semi-psychotic mortician, and they received their second windfall of the night, this time the cash buying their silence.

Timothy Eckels drove home content with a job well done, both in terms of justice and his artistry with body preparation. Working his magic on a still-living human had been different. He wasn't accustomed to warm, pliable flesh, but the thought that he was protecting Tiara had spurred him on. He was feeling on top of the world...until his phone rang.

The caller came up Unknown. Again. His jubilation doused, Tim looked at the phone, wondering if he should pick up the call. When it stopped buzzing, he breathed a sigh of relief. And then it started again. Sweat beaded on his upper lip and he swallowed hard, his heart rate accelerating.

He had to know. He couldn't leave it alone. Whoever was calling would keep trying until he picked up the phone. He pulled over to the side of the road and jabbed a finger at the green Answer button, clicking it over to speaker phone, but didn't say a word. Both parties sat in silence, listening, as seconds ticked by, then...very faintly...Tim heard...a laugh. A woman's laugh. Susannah. Click.

CHAPTER TWENTY

Now that she was close – close enough to taste it, close enough to feel his quiet presence – Susannah wanted to slow her pace. She didn't know what she wanted to do with...or, more to the point, *to* her husband. She had to see him, that was a given, but she rather enjoyed the thought of observing him, unnoticed. She wanted to watch his movements, see what he was like, if he looked different now that they'd been apart for weeks. She'd only ever known him in the context of what he was like with her, and now she'd have the chance to see how he functioned without her. She had no doubt that he could survive on his own, and that he probably actually preferred it, but she wanted to see for herself who Timothy Eckels really was.

Stopping in a thrift shop to purchase an outfit

that was a bit more conservative than the ripped jeans and black t-shirts she'd pilfered from Angelica's wardrobe, Susannah dressed in a gas station restroom and observed herself in the mirror, something she hadn't done for a long time.

She looked refreshed, despite having slept in her car for the third day in a row, and there was a gleam in her eyes and color in her cheeks that had nothing to do with the fact that her new clothes fit her so perfectly. She was in Tim's town, and it was time to put her plan together. She'd bought the outfit that she currently wore, along with several others, so that she'd fit in. She wanted to look like a clueless tourist, so that if she happened to walk by a member of law enforcement, they'd merely smile, nod, and keep going, if they noticed her at all.

Susannah had stopped into the three funeral homes listed in Key West, and had asked for Tim by name. If he had indeed worked at any of them, she'd planned to run before he could see who was inquiring after him. She was merely trying to locate him so that she'd have a location to stake out and observe his comings and goings. What she really wanted to see was where he lived. Frustrated at her lack of progress, she found herself wandering along the boardwalk, trying to think of other places where he might have tried to gain employment. He wasn't a social person, so retail, restaurant and resort options were out, which didn't leave much in the vacation playground of Key West.

Dejected, Susannah sat on the edge of the boardwalk, gazing out at the water, and noticed that there was a beach yoga class going through its routine, off to her right. A premonition of sorts tickled at the base of her spine, traveling upward to make the hairs at her nape stand on end, and she caught a flash of movement up the beach, near a stand of palms. An overly muscular body builder had fallen to the sand, clutching his crotch. Always eager to applaud the fall of the vain and arrogant, Susannah stood and crept closer, wanting to see who had taken down the bodybuilder.

Her hair stood on end, and she nearly gasped when she caught a glimpse of a paunchy, bespectacled man slipping out of sight behind the palms. Tim. She'd found him. Hurrying after him, she hung back enough that he didn't realize he was being followed. He obviously knew the area well, hurrying down alleys and between backyards, while calling no attention to himself and looking, for all intents and purposes, like he was merely a snowbird out for a stroll.

He was tanned. Her mouth went dry as she stared at him, her eyes drinking in the sight of him like a woman in the desert. As yet, she felt no murderous impulses toward him, despite the fact that he'd run away, trying to elude her.

For some reason, Tim suddenly stopped. Susannah was certain he hadn't seen her, and pretty sure that he hadn't even perceived her. He wasn't looking around with uncertainty, as her victims often did when they felt the heat of her gaze on their backs. He merely ducked between some bushes and stayed there. He wasn't hiding...he was lurking. But why? She was determined to find out, and she didn't have to wait long.

A young blonde woman – very young, college-age maybe – came walking up the sidewalk with a swaggering man who was a few years older. The two were engaged in conversation and laughter, so they never saw the still-somewhat-pallid mortician slinking along behind them. Susannah frowned. Her Timothy was clearly following this couple, but why? Forming the end of the creeper train, she kept her distance, but made certain that Tim was never out of her sight. There was a burning feeling in her chest that she didn't recognize at first, and when she finally did figure it out, it disgusted her to no end. Jealousy.

The blonde that Tim was following was younger and far more attractive than Susannah, and that twisted her gut with a fury so profound that she shook from it. Was Tim interested in this child? Was he harboring...carnal thoughts? Susannah wanted to scream, as various scenarios involving Tim and his prey flashed through her mind. In every scenario, the young woman ended up dead at her hand, which she found motivating.

How dare he? Timothy Eckels was a married man. For someone who didn't typically care too much about the behaviors of humans, other than harboring the desire to exterminate domineering males, Susannah was unnaturally bothered by the thought of her mate being interested in someone else. And that pissed her off.

She followed Tim, and saw the young woman say goodbye to her escort, entering a home on a quiet cul-de-sac. Now she knew where the young woman lived. That could come in handy. Keeping an eye on Tim, who stayed in hiding until the man who had escorted the blonde home had left the neighborhood, Susannah's heart leapt when he suddenly popped out into

211

view, moving down the sidewalk, looking as though he hadn't a care in the world. He passed by the blonde's house, pulled a key out of his pocket, and entered the house next door. Susannah now knew where her husband lived, knew where the blonde lived, and could begin stalking them both in earnest.

Susannah had almost begun to tire of watching Timothy Eckels and the two women who lived next door to him. She assumed that they were mother and daughter, though there was no discernable resemblance between them. The mother and daughter came and went pretty regularly, and their lives revolved around a pie shop across the street from the beach. Tim's life consisted mainly of following them on a fairly regular basis.

She'd nearly gotten caught watching him on one particular evening. He'd followed the daughter to a boisterous house party, and had watched the party for a while from within a clump of bushes. How this man managed to hide effectively in foliage, while never being accosted by the multitude of bugs and reptiles that resided on the island, Susannah had no idea, but then, Tim had always sort of blended into the background, so she shouldn't have been surprised.

While she was watching Tim, who was watching the party, something vile and reptilian had skittered across her hiking-sandal-clad toes, distracting her from her task and necessitating the need to hold back a bloodcurdling scream. When she looked up again from her own hiding spot, having successfully eluded the lizard, she saw Tim making a beeline toward the bushes where she'd taken refuge for her surveillance. Shimmying quickly between the bushes and a rather unforgiving fence, she'd managed to duck down just in time, while Tim scooted through the undergrowth heading the other direction. The rather large man who stumbled after him gave up, either unable or unwilling to follow the meek little man who moved like a shadow, fast and fleeting.

Aside from that encounter, Tim's experiences had been rather mundane. It surprised Susannah to learn that her husband was a voyeur of sorts. He'd never shown her that side of himself, and she wondered if he'd formed the habit after she'd been taken to jail. Then again, he could have been a stalker the entire time she'd known him, and she never would have realized it. Her own peculiar activities had consumed her attention. Truthfully, she hadn't paid much attention to the quiet man she'd married. They both seemed to prefer it that way, and now she had to wonder why he'd been so content to leave her to her own devices. Was the man who preferred the company of the dead hiding just as many secrets as she?

Tim had gone back and forth to the party house several times after he'd nearly discovered her, and she wondered what it was that fascinated him about that particular location. He'd take out a notepad and make notes about the comings and goings of the shabby homes' inhabitants, then slip away to his home. Susannah wanted that notepad so badly that it made her fingers itch. She'd gone quite some time without taking a life, and she wondered if she might be able to find justification for her cause within the pages of Tim's notes. His goal in observing this particular house, when he executed it, shocked her to her core, and made her want him like she'd never wanted him before.

Prepared for every contingency that she could imagine, Susannah had taken to parking Angelica's car a short distance away from Tim's neighborhood so that if he decided to take his stalking show on the road, she'd be able to dash to her vehicle and begin to tail him before he could make it out of his neighborhood, as long as he obeyed speed limit laws, which he almost always did. On one particular evening, a day after a disgusting display of vulgarity from a muscle-head who brought the blonde home, Tim went into the party house, and did something that Susannah would never have believed if she hadn't seen it with her very own eyes.

When she saw her husband dragging a body from the ill-kept abode, a jolt of murderously sexual pleasure surged through her like a lightning bolt. Nerve endings sizzling from head to toe, she held her breath to keep from panting, while watching Tim drag the muscle-head, whom he'd incapacitated once before - on the beach, to his car in the alley. A clump of the thinning strands of Tim's hair dangled over his sweat-drenched forehead as he wrangled the bodybuilder into his backseat, shadows growing longer in the waning sunlight.

When the former mortician returned home with his prize, he pulled the car into the garage, closing the door behind it. Susannah stashed her car in its usual spot and crept around the side of the garage, crouching beneath the garage window, which Tim had completely covered with what looked like light-blocking black fabric. She heard a sound that sent another thrill through her. After opening and closing the driver's door of the car, then opening and finally closing the door to the backseat, there were a series of thumps, a period of silence and then...Tim started humming. She'd only heard him do that on a handful of occasions. It was always when he'd had a particularly challenging reconstruction on a body... and he'd known that his expert touch was creating a masterpiece. Had Tim actually killed a man so that he could prepare his body? If so, had he chosen the bodybuilder specifically because he'd been bullied by him? If that were the case, perhaps Timothy Eckels had a value system that was morbidly similar to that of his estranged wife. The thought excited her beyond belief.

Adrenaline surging through her veins, Susannah stayed motionless below the window, seriously considering revealing herself to her husband imme-diately. Surely if he had done the thing that she'd done so many times, he couldn't sit in judgment of her. Perhaps the revelation of her dark hobby had inspired him to explore his darker side. She admired his skill with the dead, perhaps he'd admired her skill in dispatching with the living. Oh, what a couple they could be if he would give in entirely to any murderous impulses that he might have.

Susannah fantasized about the cleansing of society that they could do if they could work together as a team.

But, could she trust him? The way that he'd looked at her toward the end, when he'd begun to suspect. She'd seen judgment in those formerly accepting eyes. Had he changed his mind in her absence? Perhaps she shouldn't risk revealing her presence just yet, no matter how badly she wanted to celebrate his adventure with him. Perhaps what he did with the body once he was done with it would give her a clue as to his state of mind. She needed to know if he was going to be an asset before she considered any kind of partnership. Time would tell. For now, it would be prudent to stay in the shadows, watching.

It was more than an hour later when Tim opened and closed the car doors again. Susannah had moved from her crouched position beneath the window several times to stretch her muscles, and was relieved that her husband was going to be on the move at last. Taking a route that had become so familiar that she could practically do it with her eyes closed, she made her way back to her car and sat watching until Tim pulled out of the neighborhood.

"Where are you going, Timmy?" Susannah murmured, with a shiver of excitement.

They'd traveled beyond the benign existence of Tim's solidly middle class neighborhood and were venturing into much rougher surroundings, headed toward a fairly desolate area of the commercial docks. This was not a haven for cruise ships and tourists, this was the underbelly of the island, and Susannah was intrigued to discover what her husband was up to. She prided herself on being able to figure people out, but he'd surprised her today.

Tim's car rolled to a stop next to an area where large metal containers awaiting shipment were stacked. Susannah saw a fatal flaw in his plan. There were two unsavory characters loitering near Tim's parking spot. The mortician would never be able to hold his own against such men, and she steeled herself for the possibility that she might have to step in with her multitude of blades in order to save her husband. If anyone killed Timothy Eckels, it would be her, and given his newly-discovered propensity for dark mischief, she wasn't certain if she wanted to any longer.

Deftly, she dug into the backpack on the seat beside her, unsheathing her tools of the trade from the t-shirts she'd wrapped around them. She'd parked behind a stack of containers far enough away where she wouldn't be spotted by Tim or the thugs whom he was now approaching, much to her alarm. Carefully opening her car door, in a manner that made no sound to give away her position – she'd oiled the hinges shortly after stealing it – she squatted beside the car, peering through the darkness at her husband, knife in her belt, cleaver in her hand, ready to defend her Timmy, to the death if necessary.

Tim's posture broadcast the reality that he was not afraid of the young men with whom he was currently speaking. Susannah wondered if perhaps his mind had snapped. This was definitely a time when the mortician should be afraid, but clearly, he wasn't. He spoke with the street toughs, who appeared to be decidedly hostile at the outset, but then whom inexplicably relaxed. The conversation looked almost casual, nonthreatening, which mystified Susannah.

The reason for their amiable demeanor became clear when Tim reached into his pocket, pulled out a thick envelope and handed it to one of the thugs. The young man reached in, grabbed the contents, which turned out to be a wad of cash, and handed the envelope back to Tim with a nod. He and his buddy went to the car, opened the back door and pulled the bodybuilder out.

What Susannah saw then made her eyes go wide with admiration and the slightest tingle of horror. When the muscle-head hit the ground as Tim drove away, he began to writhe and utter eerie sounds of terror which seemed to be muted...smothered almost. She could hear that the thugs with whom Tim had left the bodybuilder were talking, and they seemed a bit surprised, but she was too far away to hear what they were saying as they stared down at the struggling man, whose feet and hands were zip-tied together.

Shaking his head, one of the young men shrugged and kicked the trussed-up body builder in the ribs, eliciting another high-pitched, smothered cry from him. Susannah's curiosity overcame her good sense. She had to see what her Timmy had done. The thought of what might have happened titillated her to no end, but she had to be sure. Rising to her feet, cleaver displayed prominently in her hand, Susannah walked boldly toward the odd trio. The eyes of all three immediately went to the glint of her weapon when she approached.

A smile stretched across her features. A wicked, vulgar smile full of dark glee.

He'd done it. Her Timmy had surprised her yet again, and his simple act left her yearning for him so powerfully that she ached.

The look on her face, combined with the rather large meat cleaver in her hand, inspired curiosity in the thugs, and the taller of the two acknowledged her with an upward jerk of his chin. Susannah kept smiling and squatted next to the terrorized muscle-head.

"Perfect work, as always," she whispered, running her finger along his glued-together lips. "No wonder you couldn't scream," she chuckled.

"Hey Red, what you lookin' for tonight?" the young man who'd acknowledged her asked.

Still amused by the fact that Tim had prepared a living human being just like he prepared the dead, right down to the flawless makeup job, Susannah stood and turned toward the thugs, light from a nearly full moon glinting on the blade of her cleaver.

"You better not be thinking about using that," the other tough said, eyeing the deadly kitchen tool.

"I don't think you're in a position to be making threats," Susannah said simply, dismissing him and focusing on his friend. "You guys wanna make some money?" she asked.

"That's why we're here. What kind of fix you need, lady?" he started digging in his pockets.

"I don't do drugs," Susannah rolled her eyes.

Drugs clouded the senses. She preferred to be in control. Of everything. Always.

"What you want then?" the tall guy frowned, his eyes darting down to the hand that held the cleaver.

The other punk put a hand on his zipper.

"No, I definitely don't want that," Susannah made a face.

"Then what?" the tall guy stepped toward her.

"Him," she gestured at the bound man with the cleaver.

"Why?" thug two dropped his hand from his zipper.

"Gotta have a souvenir to take home from my vacation in the Keys, right?" Susannah snickered.

The two toughs didn't find that funny. She could tell that she was freaking them out a bit.

"How much you got?" tall guy decided to get to the bottom line.

Susannah always carried at least a hundred dollars in the pocket of her pants. You never knew when it might come in handy. She reached in and pulled out a wad of bills. Tall guy nodded.

"Put him in my car and it's yours," she promised, turning and heading toward her car.

The toughs exchanged a look, the tall one shrugged and they bent to pick up the again-squalling bodybuilder. Susannah opened the back door of her car and they threw him in. She handed the tall one the money and tapped the bodybuilder on the forehead with the handle of the meat cleaver.

"Hush," she ordered, but the keening sound he'd been uttering continued. "Can one of you boys knock him out for me?" she sighed.

Thug two smirked and went to the car, where he punched the bodybuilder in the face, knocking him out cold.

"Nice shot," Susannah nodded. "Too bad you messed his makeup up," she looked down at him ruefully.

"So, what you gonna do with him?" tall guy asked.

"Have a little fun. What were you guys gonna do with him?" she asked, curious as to what deal Timmy had made with them.

Tall guy shrugged.

"Rough him up. Maybe throw him in the water."

"It'd be kind of hard to swim in his condition," Susannah observed.

"Ain't our problem," thug two shot back.

Susannah smiled, admiring his spirit, even if she would like to take his attitude down a notch by removing a body part or two.

"Have a nice evening gentlemen," she replied, getting into the car. As she was pulling away, she gave them one final thought. "Oh, and by the way... in case you thought of reporting this little exchange, or the one you had before it...your fingerprints are now all over my car. Take care," she smiled, gave them a little wave, and sped away.

CHAPTER TWENTY-ONE

Tim's elation at having completed his dark objective had been more than dimmed by the chilling phone call that he'd received on the way home. He drove into his garage and sat in his car, listening to the soft ticking of his engine as it cooled in the silence. Susannah.

He'd tried so hard to run away, not only from the danger of her, but from the memories of her. Their whole life together had been a lie, and all he wanted to do was forget, but she wouldn't let him. What did her sinister laugh mean? Realistically speaking, it meant that she hadn't yet been caught. Was she looking for him? Had she found him? Was she right now lurking in the unlit confines of his living room? There, among the preserved creatures that he'd memorialized? He had to admit to himself that he didn't want to find out, but he couldn't sit here in the garage all night. A bead of sweat trickled down his temple, tracing a cold path in front of his ear, and down to his neck. He swiped it impatiently away before it could soak into his collar. His stomach churned as he thought of his wife.

Susannah may have been gone for weeks, but she haunted him still, and he resented her for that. He bore her no ill will, but if it came down to it, he'd have no qualms about turning her over to the authorities. What he'd done to Tiara's would-be-rapist was assault, at worst. What Susannah did... killing innocent people and turning their skin into leaves to hang on her tree sculpture made of bones, was an abomination. She was evil, she was sick, and inexplicably, she was still his problem.

Maybe she was inside. Maybe she was crouched in a dark corner between the house and the garage waiting for him. Maybe...if she was there, and if she meant him harm...maybe she'd at least have the dignity to kill him quickly. He'd suffered enough on her account. Would she have the integrity to at least let him die on his own terms? Somehow, he doubted it. What she'd done to her victims went far beyond the mere act of killing, and Tim had no reason to believe that their brief marriage would compel her to be compassionate with him.

"This is ridiculous," he muttered, shaking his head and trying to will himself to get out of the car.

His fingers remained firmly clamped around the steering wheel.

"If I die, I die," he sighed finally, grasping the door handle before he could change his mind.

He opened the door quietly, and got out, closing it gently, wincing when it clicked shut. Tim froze in place, listening. He heard nothing but the sound of distant traffic, and made his way silently to the door which led outside. In order to get to the house, he had to cross a darkened area of the yard and either make his way to the front door or the back, a daunting trek in light of his shattered nerves.

He'd made two steps toward the house when a figure shot out from under the bushes and darted straight at him.

"Maisie!" he whispered hoarsely, his hand to his thumping chest.

The little cat had terrified him, but she couldn't have known. He bent and picked up the purring creature, scratching between her eyes to soothe his jangled nerves, and a horrifying thought crossed his mind. How had the cat gotten outside? She'd been inside when he left. She never went outside other than to do her business, and he would never have left her out when he knew he wasn't going to be home. Tim stood rooted to the spot, wondering what to do. If Susannah was in his house, which was a strange thought to have, since there was no way that she could possibly know where he was, he didn't want her to know that he had a cat. Goodness only knows what she might do to the poor innocent creature if she thought that she could lash out at him through the animal. He dropped Maisie like she was on fire, eliciting an offended meow from the tiny feline.

"Shh..." he cautioned with a whisper, listening in the darkness, which suddenly felt heavy around him.

He took one step at a time, pausing after each one, getting closer and closer to the house. When he reached his front door, his heart hammered in his throat as he noted that it was ajar. All of the lights in the house were off, and he didn't hear a sound, though he was quite certain that anyone who may have been inside could hear the pulsing of blood which was currently shooting through his veins like whitewater. Tim was cold, despite the balmy evening, and he broke out in nervous sweat. He could smell it seeping from his pores, heralding his presence in a most vile manner. The smell of fear, it disgusted him.

Something broke free within Timothy Eckels just then. He was tired of being toyed with, tired living in fear, and tired of allowing a lying psychopath to manipulate his existence. He shoved the door open and flipped on the lights, his eyes having a hard time adjusting the dramatic change.

"Here I am," he announced loudly, slamming the front door shut, eyes blazing behind his thick glasses. "Here I am," he barked again, storming down the hall to check the bedrooms and bathrooms for the presence of an unwanted visitor.

Chest heaving, teeth clenched in fury, he stood in the middle of his bedroom and listened. Nothing. Then...a door slammed. The back door. Charging through the kitchen, he hollered.

"Who are you? What do you want?" he raged, running as fast as his legs would carry him.

He flung open the door to the back porch and charged out into the yard, promptly tripping over a potted plant that was in his path. Had he left it there? In his terror, he couldn't remember. He fell to the ground with a loud whump, and groaned, squinting into the darkness, hoping to catch a glimpse of his tormentor. This was so like Susannah. She was a cruel child with a magnifying glass, and he was the bug that she tormented, burning him little by little until he turned to ash.

With a disgusted grunt, he hove himself to his feet, brushed off his trousers and limped back to the house. Once inside, he stood in the kitchen, trying to catch his breath and processing what had just happened. Tim snapped on the kitchen light, and when his eyes adjusted, he began to move through the house, his eyes darting to every corner, his mind hearing sounds that had never entered his ears. He was jumping at shadows and he thought dark thoughts about his wife for continuing to cause him grief. He wondered if he was losing his mind, as he dashed from room to room, looking in closets and under furnishings like a madman.

Once he'd calmed down enough to think more rationally, Tim realized that the odds against his intruder being his estranged wife were astronomical. More likely, the lout who had tried to accost Tiara had peeled his eyes and lips open and was out for revenge. Tim hadn't really thought that one through. He figured that the young men at the docks would have roughed him up enough to teach him a lesson. Then a most unsettling thought occurred to him.

He'd come directly home from the docks. Aside from pulling to the side of the road briefly, to answer his phone, he'd wasted no time. It would have been impossible for the bodybuilder to free himself and get to Tim's house before he did.

Perhaps it could've been the unfortunate jerk's roommates...but how would they have even known what happened yet? Tim frowned. Could it have been random? Why would a garden variety burglar come in and take nothing? Had Tim gotten home just in time? As much as he hated to admit it, Tim had to concede that the possibility that it was Susannah who had come into his home was remote, but...still possible. He swallowed hard, then sighed. It would do him no good to dwell on what might be, and he had absolutely no desire to call the police, so he might as well continue to explore his violated space, looking for clues as to who his intruder may have been.

After a thorough inspection of the house, which turned up a whole lot of nothing, Tim pulled the trash out from under his kitchen sink, tied up the bag and tossed it onto the back porch, not really wanting to go wandering about in the dark at the moment. Stepping onto the porch, he called to his cat, having forgotten that she was still outside.

"Maisie," he called. "Here kitty, kitty."

Silence. No rustling in the grass, no petite cat slinking out from under a bush.

"Maisie?" Tim said again, trying not to become alarmed.

He walked out into the backyard, calling her name and looking in all of her usual resting places. When he didn't find her, he made his way around the side of the house and into the front yard. No Maisie. He checked the opposite side of the house. Same result. When he came back around to the front, he looked over at the garage and saw that the garage door was ajar. Had he left it that way when he came in? He was so focused on listening, that he couldn't remember. Could the intruder be hiding in there? Perhaps Maisie had butted her head against the door and opened it.

"Maisie?" Tim said, hating that his voice trembled a bit.

He walked toward the garage. No movement, no sound. He reached the door. Putting the palm of his hand flat against it, he pushed gently. There was a creaking groan as it swung open.

"Go big or go home," he muttered, reaching for the garage light and flipping it on.

Everything was the same as it was when he last

saw it, as far as he could tell. He peeked in the car windows and saw nothing amiss. He was about to turn out the light and head back to the house, when something on his workbench caught his eye. There was a small, dark pile of something on his normally immaculate work area. His stomach dropped, and for a moment, he hesitated near the door. Curiosity overcame reticence, however, and he slowly approached the bench.

Hair. It was a clump of hair. Conor's hair. Had Tim left it there? Had he been so preoccupied that he'd missed it when he cleaned up after his dirty deed? That had to be the answer, which infuriated him. Timothy Eckels prided himself on very few things, but among them were cleanliness and attention to detail. The thought that Susannah was still affecting him so profoundly that he'd allowed himself to become that distracted, caused the flame of his resentment to burn white-hot. He refused to touch Conor's hair with his ungloved hands, so he brushed at it with a hand broom that hung above the workbench, sweeping it into the trash. Tomorrow he'd burn it, but tonight, he planned to have a hot cup of tea to settle his nerves and turn in for the night.

He closed and locked the garage, entirely

unaware that his teeth were still clamped firmly together, which would later result in a screaming headache. He also completely forgot that he'd come outside originally to look for Maisie, who was still nowhere to be found. He'd never left her outside overnight, but tonight, when he flopped into bed, still seething, he gave no thought to the furry creature who normally slept on the pillow beside him.

CHAPTER TWENTY-TWO

Susannah decided that it was time to play some sweetly sadistic games. On some level, she wanted to punish her Timmy for paying so much attention to the neighbor ladies, and she also wanted to take the ladies themselves down a notch. With a little luck and some seriously diabolical planning, she could kill both of those birds with one stone, figuratively speaking.

She'd taken the unfortunate bodybuilder on a whim, and now she didn't quite know what to do with him. She could kill him, but since she didn't really know if he was actually arrogant or domineering, she couldn't quite feel good about that. He didn't have any interesting tattoos or skin features that she wanted to harvest – beer signs, team logos and car ads weren't her style - and his hair was merely ordinary. There was also the issue of disposing of a body in an unfamiliar place, where she didn't have any dump sites. Killing him would be inconvenient. Perhaps she could use him to make a statement.

Susannah was quite certain that Tim had counted on the street toughs eliminating the body-builder. How would he react if the muscle-head showed up a bit traumatized, but otherwise relatively unscathed? Wouldn't it be kind of fun to terrorize her mischievous husband like a rat in a horrific maze, where fear lurked around every corner? If she could put him into a perpetual state of paranoia, would it push him even further over the edge? Far enough, maybe, to convince him to join her in pursuit of her hobby? It was worth a shot.

"Be free, dumb beefcake," Susannah whispered, using her knife to cut the zip ties from his hands and feet.

She was in no danger. He couldn't see or speak, and it was the middle of the night. She was kind enough to dump him in his backyard, so that his roommates could discover him at some point. He'd survive. He might need some serious therapy, but he'd survive. She smiled as she drove away, her mind filled with ideas as to how she could torment Timmy and his neighbors.

Susannah had been watching Tim for long enough that she'd had the opportunity to observe the habits of his neighbors as well. The daughter apparently didn't live with her mother, but stayed over often enough, and when she did, they generally left the house together each morning, not returning until six o'clock or after. The mother's house was empty pretty much all day, every day, which left lots of opportunities for a bit of scary mischief. She had to be careful though. While their routine was supremely predictable, Tim's was a bit less so. He still watched Tiara as she came and went, but during the bulk of the day, he often puttered around at home.

Susannah knew that he'd be watching the neighbor's house when he was home, which would make getting in and out of it much trickier. That thought made her giggle a bit. If she could make Tim think that he'd seen her, it would make him supremely uncomfortable, and he wouldn't even be able to warn the women next door about his notorious wife. That kind of chafing discomfort was part of her goal.

She knew that the mother locked up before she left every morning, so there'd be no open doors for her to just stroll through. She might have to get creative. Her lock-picking skills weren't great, and she didn't want to leave any evidence of forced entry. It would also be fun to get a phone number and start making some disturbing phone calls to the gals. In the meantime, she suddenly had the craving for some pie.

After establishing that Tim was still in his house after the two women next door left for the day, Susannah took her time, meandering down to the beach. She was decked out in her 'I'm a non-descript tourist' gear, and hoped to get an up-close and personal encounter with one or both of Tim's neighbors. She'd also like to sample their pie to see if they could actually bake. If she saw green Key Lime pie, she might just throw it at them. Everyone who knew their way around a kitchen knew that real Key Lime pie was pale in color, not neon green.

There was a line that ran out the door of the busy pie shop, which suited Susannah's purpose perfectly. She would blend in much better as part of a crowd. The exterior of the building was a lime green splash of color that was mildly off-putting, but the garish mermaids cavorting on the walls inside the shop made Susannah wrinkle her nose in distaste. Of course the two women would be whimsical. Whimsy made her shudder. She sincerely hoped that they took their food production far more seriously than they took their décor.

The world around Susannah slowed, and her focus narrowed when she stepped inside the small shop. There, behind the cash register was the blonde with whom Tim seemed to be so fascinated. Her smile was brave, but harried, as she dealt with customer after customer. The background noise faded to oblivion as the killer focused on the young woman's features. As if she'd felt the burning gaze, the blonde looked up, met Susannah's eyes, though she was behind several customers, and faltered a bit in her attempt to smile, instead cocking her head and frowning slightly, before going back to the next person in line. Susannah dropped her gaze immediately, not wanting to bring undue attention to herself. There had been intelligence in the blonde's gaze, which bothered her. It was much easier to think that the object of her Timmy's attention had been merely a bubbleheaded beach bunny. This young woman might be a force to contend with, which would make her demise that much sweeter.

"Hi, what can I get for you today?" she asked, with forced cheerfulness, as Susannah fixated on her name tag.

Tiara? Really? Who names their child Tiara? Was mommy's name Princess?

"Can I help you?" Tiara asked, a bit louder this time, snapping Susannah out of her mocking daze.

"Oh, yes," Susannah pasted on a plastic smile, noting that the Key Lime pie in the case was the appropriate color. "I'd like a piece of Key Lime pie, please."

"For here or to go?" Tiara punched numbers into the old-fashioned register.

"To go," Susannah replied immediately.

The thought of sitting down in the overcrowded shop, being immersed in the inane chatter of morning pie-eaters was shudder-inducing. She could take her pie outside and observe the shop from a better, and far quieter vantage point.

Tiara took her money, handed back her change and began to plate the pie, but stared at Susannah for a moment.

"Have we met before?" she asked, handing over the decadent-looking slice of pie, in a pie shaped plastic container.

Susannah's throat constricted, but she kept her facial expression neutral.

"I don't think so. I hear that all the time though. Guess I just have one of those faces," she shrugged, hoping she looked nonchalant, despite the fact that her heart was racing.

"Guess so," Tiara sounded uncertain, but handed her a plastic packet containing a fork and a paper napkin. "Anyway, have a nice day," she dismissed her, shifting her gaze to the next customer.

Susannah had a sudden impulse to remove the blonde's eyeballs with the plastic fork. Jealousy was an ugly monster. She walked away without saying another word. Seating herself on a park bench across the street, she sank her flimsy fork into the pie. She bought it, so she might as well eat it, besides, her curiosity was killing her. It was perfect. A magically smooth consistency, the proper balance of tart and sweet, the flaky crust...the only better pie she'd ever had was...Tim's. She experienced a momentary pang of sentimental nonsense, remembering the two of them having dinner for the very first time. She'd invited him over, he'd brought a luscious pie. She'd actually been comfortable, for the first time ever, in the presence of a human whom she didn't want to kill. Oh, how their lives had changed since then.

Shaking off the mantle of despondency that threatened to smother her in emotion, Susannah discovered that she couldn't stomach another bite of the nearly perfect pie, and tossed it in a nearby trash can. She hated being wasteful, but when she thought about the hands that had prepared the treat, it turned her stomach. Tiara's careless dismissal of her made her fury grow, and she realized that she didn't want to just kill either of the two women right away. She wanted to make them suffer. She wanted them to cringe inside their home like mice under the shadow of a circling hawk. She wanted them to quiver and despair, and then maybe die. She hadn't made up her mind yet, which was curious. Typically, she was quite certain about the dilemma of 'to kill or not to kill,' but she'd been wishy-washy lately, a fact that she blamed on Tim. He hadn't behaved as expected, and it had thrown her off her game a bit. She had to regain the upper hand, or she'd be most out of sorts.

Susannah was just about to leave, planning on beginning her period of torment, when she saw Tim round the corner, headed for the pie shop. Why did her heart always leap to her throat at the sight of him? She wasn't some lovesick teenager for crying out loud. She stood and stared, daring him to see her, and just as he opened the door to the shop, he stopped. And stared. At her.

Heart pounding, she knew that he had to be

quite confused right about now. Her hair was short and red, not long and blonde, and she'd lost more than twenty pounds, tightening up the flesh on her compact frame by eating sporadically and staying in peak physical condition. Tim's eyes were weak. He used a magnifier even with his glasses when he was preparing the dead. He couldn't actually see well enough, with her standing across the street, to be certain that it was her. But, maybe he felt it? Maybe he knew on a level that transcended physical sight? The thought made her smile.

If he did think that he saw her, it would make it even easier for her to crawl into his psyche and shred it. She wanted him to doubt his sanity. She wanted him to question everything, including his own miserable existence. What she wasn't honest enough to admit, even to herself, was that she desperately wanted him...to need her.

She'd have time to analyze her odd mix of feelings towards her husband later, but now, while he and his neighbors were preoccupied with their nearly perfect pie, it was time for action. Disappearing around the side of a building, so that if Tim looked across the street again, it would seem that she had vanished into thin air, she jogged at an easy pace, headed for their neighborhood.

As she'd suspected, both the back door and the front door at Tim's neighbor's house were locked, as was the patio door. The bathroom window, however was open about an inch and had no screen. Getting in would be like taking candy from a baby, but way more satisfying. Using gloves that she'd brought with her, Susannah pushed up the window, hoisted herself up, and slipped inside, thankful that the yard was shaded on all sides by bushes and trees, obscuring the view.

The bathroom was tidy, but by no means immaculate, as was the rest of the house, with one exception. The mother, whose name was Marilyn, Susannah soon found out, had a home office that was immaculate. Not a particle of dust nor scrap of paper dared to defile the pristine space. Everything was perfectly in place. The stapler was exactly parallel to the computer keyboard and the tape dispenser. The pad of sticky notes was not folded up at the corners and no impressions from having written on it were present. Bills and other papers were filed in labeled folders, which might come in handy, and a handful of sharpened pencils, all the same height, graced the pencil holder.

Susannah moved everything to the exact opposite side of the desk that it had been on. The stapler moved from the far right to the far left, and everything else was switched out as well. Pressing hard on the pad of sticky notes, she drew a whimsical smiley face, which seemed sinister, even to her, and tore off the note, sticking it on the screen of the recently-moved computer. Crookedly.

There was a file folder labeled 'Personal' and she shuffled it behind a folder labeled 'Taxes,' giggling all the while. There was nothing remarkable about Marilyn's room, but Susannah tore the coppery strands of hair out of Marilyn's brush and scattered them on her ivory satin bedspread, just to make her paranoid.

The room that Tiara obviously stayed in when she visited her mother was a bit of a mess, but Susannah found a faded blue sweatshirt on the floor that she liked, so she tied it around her waist to take with her. Going to the kitchen, she filled the sugar bowl with salt, squirted catsup in the milk carton, and added potting soil to the freshly ground coffee that was in a container by the coffee pot.

"My work here is done," she grinned slyly.

She went back toward the bathroom, planning to leave the same way that she'd come in, so that if Tim happened to be spying on his neighbors, he wouldn't see her. She'd just entered the hall when she heard a key in the front door lock, and barely had time to dart into the bathroom before Tiara opened it. The kid had deviated from her usual pattern, and Susannah cursed inwardly. She only had a small knife with her. She could use it to kill, but it would be awkward and messy. Besides, killing one of Tim's neighbors would tip him off that she actually was in town, and she wasn't quite ready for that confirmation, despite the clues that she was leaving.

Hearing footsteps coming down the hall toward the bathroom, Susannah slipped into the bathtub, thankful that the curtain surrounding it wasn't transparent. The footsteps grew closer, and Tiara came into the bathroom. Susannah held her breath, her ass clenched so tightly that she couldn't have fit a dime between them. The footsteps just stopped. Susannah stared at the shower curtain, feeling the presence of the young woman on the other side of it and wondering why she wasn't doing anything. Had she been heard? Did Tiara know?

A drawer opened, and she heard slow pull of a brush being run through silky blonde strands that she wanted to rip out one by one. There was the clunk of the brush going back into the drawer and another agonizing silence. A sigh. If Tiara suspected anything, she wasn't showing it. The shower curtain fluttered as she moved through the room. Finally, the blessed sound of footsteps leaving the room. Susannah waited. The refrigerator opened and closed, and she knew it was time to make her move. The kitchen was on the other end of the house, so she'd have less chance of being heard.

She opened the bathroom window, hoisted herself up and lowered herself down, carefully, dropping the last six inches or so. When her feet hit the ground, she wasn't counting on the gopher hole that her heel landed in, and she twisted her ankle hard. Stumbling, she landed against the pastel siding with a thunk. With a startled gasp, she flattened herself against the side of the house, under the window, as she heard footsteps pounding into the bathroom. Susannah hadn't had time to pull the window shut, and she was quite certain that if Tiara leaned out of it at all, she'd be spotted. Heart thumping so loudly that she'd feared it would be heard from inside the bathroom, Susannah didn't move a muscle, even when a fat bumblebee buzzed lazily around her face, briefly lighting on her nose, which tickled abominably.

"What the heck was that?" she heard Tiara mutter.

Suddenly, the window above her made a

creaking noise. Oh god, was Tiara about to look out? Susannah squeezed her eyes shut and waited, her teeth clenched in frustration. The window slid shut. Tiara hadn't been curious enough to look outside apparently. The killer below the window went limp with relief. It wasn't Tiara's time. Yet. Swatting at the bumblebee, she counted to two hundred, then went on her way, slinking into the bushes.

She was irritated that she'd almost gotten caught, but the knowledge that Marilyn and Tiara would be in quite the tizzy, after discovering her mischief, lifted Susannah's spirits considerably.

Tim's house was locked up tight, making her wonder if he was already starting to become paranoid. Since she'd taken so much time at Marilyn's house, she wanted to get out of the area before Tim wandered home and caught her. Rather than breaking a window or forcing entry some other way, she decided to mess with his mind by exterior means. There was a potted plant on the front porch. Reaching into the pot, she grabbed a handful of soil and sprinkled it, in a serpentine trail, from the pot to the door. That would give him pause. Satisfied with her work for the day, she stood, peering around a tree in his side yard, waiting for him to return.

When she caught sight of him, she wiggled the

fronds of the nearest palmetto to capture his attention, then stepped out just far enough for him to see something that looked human. Once he started jogging toward her, eyes agoggle, she darted out of sight and easily outran him, leaving him standing in an alley huffing and puffing and undoubtedly wondering if he was seeing things.

It was a good day, and it filled her heart with glee to think of the fun that she could have once darkness fell.

CHAPTER TWENTY-THREE

Tim hadn't slept well, and a series of events had him wondering whether he might, in fact, be losing his mind. The specter of his wife hung about him like a cloud, and he constantly glanced over his shoulder, expecting to see her. There was the uncanny experience he'd had at the pie shop, when he'd caught a glimpse of someone across the street who had eerily, inexplicably reminded him of her, despite the fact that her body and hair looked nothing like Susannah. Then, when he'd come home, he could have sworn that he'd seen someone peering out at him from behind the bushes. He'd charged toward the person, seeing nothing and nearly giving himself a heart attack from the strenuous activity, coupled with the adrenaline that coursed through his veins.

Was all of this a side effect of his recent prank?

Was some form of latent guilt about what he'd done to the bodybuilder weighing so heavily upon him that he was imagining Susannah as his own personal boogeyman? He sincerely hoped that was the case.

Tim's hand shook from the combination of exertion and nerves, as he took his keys out of his pocket and went to open the door. Before he stepped up onto his porch, he noticed a perfectly serpentine trail of dirt, leading to the door. He halted, staring down at the trail. How had that happened, and what did it mean? More importantly, what should he do? He was so confused, that he literally stepped up onto the porch and scattered some of the soil with the toe of his shoe to make sure that he wasn't seeing things. He couldn't go on like this. He suddenly realized that whatever was going to happen would happen and he needed to just live his life. He needed to find a job, so that he didn't have the time to dwell on his fears. He'd bought a newspaper earlier that morning, and he vowed to spend some time combing through the want-ads once he'd had a few minutes to try to slow his heart rate and return to some semblance of normalcy.

Tim stared at the pages of the newspaper blankly, his mind a million miles away. What if he went to the police, and told them his suspicions?

Would they then detain him for questioning, because he had run? Had he made himself look guilty by fleeing from the stares and whispers of hometown folk once Susannah had been exposed? He'd done nothing wrong, but his reaction to his circumstances would make law enforcement look twice at him. And there was a fairly good chance that they wouldn't even believe him. Really, what evidence did he have to back up his suspicions that his wife was in the area? Nothing. Zip. Zilch. Zero. He'd sound like a raving mad accomplice if he tried to broach the subject to the police. Timothy Eckels knew one thing as sure as he knew his own name. He wouldn't last very long in prison. He'd been teased, mocked and abused his entire life, and he'd found his own ways to exact revenge. That wouldn't be an option in a prison setting.

He'd seen evidence of Susannah's work, though he hadn't realized it at the time. As early as his cadaver lab in college, he'd run into human remains that had leaf-shaped pieces of skin cut from them. Susannah collected the leaves, dried them and made them into macabre sculptures. They had just looked like leather, or sometimes thick paper. He hadn't realized. Who would've even thought to do such a thing? Tim's wife was quiet, sometimes brooding, but he never would have guessed at her dark hobby.

He'd only begun to suspect when he'd found hairs that were incredibly similar to a body he'd just processed, on her favorite sweater. He'd begun to wonder about the food that she prepared, and about what she did for hours on end when she was either out of the house, or in her basement workshop, a place where he was not allowed to tread.

And she had known. She must've seen it in his eyes, because her manner toward him changed. He was accustomed to an air of indifference from her, and was completely content to deal with that, but her behavior became confrontational, suspicious, and, that, he couldn't tolerate. She'd raised her voice a few times, which offended him to no end. There was no reason to behave so boorishly. His had been a quiet existence before he met her, and he'd planned to spend the rest of his days that way.

Then his world turned upside down. Susannah had been found, holding a bloody knife, in the home of a prominent veterinarian in town, who had just become a fresh corpse. She'd been captured without a whole lot of fuss, and the police had underestimated her. While they confiscated mounds of evidence from the Eckels' basement, Susannah sat in a small town jail cell. One female officer had guarded her, and somehow that officer had met a gruesome end, leaving Susannah a free, if haunted, woman.

Tim had been disgusted by his wife's hobby, and appalled that she was capable of such violence. He had a great deal of respect for the dead, but he had no interest in stocking his own trade, as it were. He remembered that she would come back after being gone for long periods of time, usually in the evening, and would demand sexual satisfaction from him. He never saw much point to the purely physical act, but, fulfilling his duties as a husband, he always obliged.

There was a wild look in her eyes during those times, and he often felt as though she was practically humming with a barely contained energy. It scared him a bit, but he allowed her to punish his body to satisfy hers, and afterward, they'd both drop into an exhausted sleep. She was fierce, and she was not to be denied. He wondered how she was satisfying those urges now, but then pushed the thoughts from his mind, as uncomfortable scenarios presented themselves in rapid succession.

Timothy Eckels wasn't typically one for introspection, but lately he'd found himself wondering why he'd ever gotten involved with a woman in the first place. His mother had abandoned him. His grandmother had raised him well, but wasn't exactly affectionate, and he'd never had what could be called an entirely positive relationship with a female in his entire life. Girls hadn't bothered with the strange, pale boy, and he'd been fine with that. Susannah had sought him out. Had seen something in him that appealed to her, and that bothered him now. What on earth was so wrong with him that he'd been the mate of choice for a serial killer?

Giving up on trying to find a job – it was an exercise in futility at the moment – he laid his head down on the table, exhausted, even though it wasn't quite noon. He fell asleep, and was oblivious to the presence of another person slipping, silent as death, into his home. This is what happens when one forgets to lock the door behind themselves.

CHAPTER TWENTY-FOUR

Susannah had waited half an hour before venturing back to Tim's house. All was quiet as she lurked in the bushes, so she decided to be a bit bolder. If Tim happened to see her, it would add to his paranoia, and if he decided to chase her, there was no way that the paunchy mortician could catch her, so her danger, both of exposure and capture, was minimal. She peeped into the kitchen window and saw nothing. Skulking along the side of the house, she then peered into the dining room window, and saw a wonderful sight. Tim, slumped over at the table, fast asleep. Her heart beat fast as she observed the somnolent form of her husband. She was so close to him. Closer than she'd been in a very long time, and the simple proximity made her quiver. She was charged with a powerful energy that she couldn't interpret clearly. Did she want to kill him, or did she merely want him?

For the moment, she'd be content to toy with him. Either way, whether he died slowly and in agony, or became her literal partner in crime, she wanted to punish him for leaving her, doubting her...rejecting her. Of all people, she'd never dreamed that Timothy Eckels would discard her like the rest of the world always had. He'd seemed special, but in that regard, he was apparently as weak as the rest of humanity. Was that weakness deserving of death? That was yet to be determined. Maybe she'd have him and then kill him. Now there was a titillating idea...

Slinking around to the front of the house, she stepped up onto the porch, and when she noticed that her dirt trail had been disturbed, a smile broke over her face like the sun. Reaching for the door-knob with a gloved hand, she turned it, elated when it opened. Despite her slow and careful entry, the door creaked when she opened it, the sound shattering the tomblike silence in Tim's house. Wincing, she froze in place, listening. No movement, no other sound.

Susannah didn't risk pushing the door shut, opting instead to leave it hanging open behind her as she ventured further into the oddly decorated home, which was filled with the end results of Tim's taxidermy hobby. Beady, plastic eyes watched her every move as she slunk through the space. She wanted to decapitate them all, and disassemble them, leaving tiny body parts scattered about, but her purpose here was to simultaneously learn more about her Timmy's current existence, while doing a few things designed specifically to freak him out. She could wreak havoc with his 'pets' another day.

Tiptoeing into the dining room, she heard a familiar sound that stopped her in her tracks. The heavy in and out of Tim's breathing. It was a sound he made only when he was in the throes of exhaustion. This meant a couple of things. One, he was sound asleep, and likely would be for a while, and two, he wouldn't wake easily, which meant that she could get into all manner of mischief with minimal risk.

The sound of him, the scent of him, which teased at her nose, even at a distance, the very presence of him, made her insides shake with longing. A still as-yet undetermined longing. She swallowed, feeling a pang of...something. Regret? Empathy? Surely not. She shook the feeling off and concentrated on the task at hand.

Aside from the menagerie of lifeless animals, the home was sparsely furnished, with no frivolous décor. Susannah moved through, glancing about, and making small changes which would make her husband question his memory, and hopefully his sanity. In rooms where blinds were closed, she opened them, and in rooms where they were open, she closed them. She opened closet doors and moved his toothbrush, after running it around the inside of the toilet bowl. In an ultimate act of desecration, she flipped the roll of toilet paper over so that it unrolled from the bottom rather than the top.

The things that Susannah was doing, as she moved swiftly through the home, were all little things when taken alone, but the combination of them could provide some taxing mental questioning from her beleaguered mate. The kitchen was too close to the dining room, where Tim was still snoozing, so she couldn't do much in there. She did, however, find an entire berry pie on the counter, which she would take with her when she left. After moving a few more objects around, and ripping the head off of a perfectly preserved kitten which had peered down at her from the top of the refrigerator, she picked up the pie, and froze in place, her heart racing.

The sound. The rise and fall of Tim's chest. She couldn't hear it.

She held her own breath, jaws clenched, and waited. If he had awoken and was seconds from seeing her, she'd have to make him decide whether he lived or died, based on his behavior and answers to her questions. It seemed like an eternity had passed when she finally heard the snort of a snore, along with a soft, unintelligible utterance, which clued her in to the fact that Tim still slumbered on.

Relief flooded through her and spurred her to depart. There would be time for more shenanigans later. She had quite a bit of money left, thanks to the generosity of the Chicago starving artists, and her room at a nearby fleabag motel had allowed her to lay low, paying in cash, under an assumed name. Living near the beach wasn't bad, and she had to admit, she was thoroughly enjoying toying with Timmy and his neighbors. Like a cat playing with a mouse, she was merely making her prey scramble and worry before she mercifully ended their misery.

Taking the pie with her, she simply walked out the front door, cut through Tim's side yard, and made her way back to the motel, where she planned out Phase Two of her torment. She had to raise the stakes in order to really get Tim's attention.

Susannah had seen a Get Well Soon bouquet delivered to Marilyn's home, on a day when Marilyn went to work by herself and Tiara didn't emerge for her daily yoga class. She hadn't thought much about it, people get sick all of the time, but now she had a use for that tidbit of information.

The pie that she had snatched from Tim's counter was a luscious-looking berry pie of some sort, which drooled bright purple juices from the evenly-spaced slits in its center. The fact that there were slits in the top would suit her purposes perfectly.

It was an odd assortment of items that Susannah purchased at a drug store near the motel. A box of hair dye - she was going with brown this time, rather than red, so that if Tim spotted her again, he'd be even more confused – a bottle of clear, tasteless laxative, and a small pediatric syringe, designed to shoot meds directly into the back of the throats of squirming, uncooperative tots.

Taking her items home, she went to work on Phase Two with savage glee. At the very least, the amount of laxative that she was about to put into the pie would send Marilyn and Tiara to the bathroom for a good part of a day, at best, it could cause kidney failure and kill them. She'd be fine with either option, though she didn't want her Timmy to go to jail. It would be much harder to drive him insane if he was incarcerated. The thought that he'd notice that his pie had gone missing made her giggle.

Loading up the syringe with laxative, she squirted it into the pie again and again, until she'd used up nearly the entire bottle. The pie's juice had largely been cooked out, and the addition of the laxative merely made it seem more juicy and luscious. While pleased at the result, Susannah felt slightly nauseated when she visualized the plump berries and flaky crust being consumed by Tiara and Marilyn. Their enjoyment of the dish that Tim had made with his own hands would be short-lived, however.

Susannah's plan was to place the pie on the counter in Marilyn's house, after mother and daughter left for work. She'd spotted a typewriter when she'd spent time in Marilyn's office, on which she planned to type a note from Tim, expressing his concern for Tiara's health and well-being, after her recent challenges. This would cause all kinds of fun drama, which she'd hopefully be able to witness from her hiding spot in Tim's yard.

———

Susannah waited impatiently for Tim to follow Marilyn and Tiara when they left the house the next morning, but the tired mortician was taking his time. She had to wonder if he was altering his routine to throw her off. He had to suspect that she was messing with him, by now. Perhaps he was even trying to figure out a way to set a trap? She had to chuckle at that. It would be a bit like the mouse setting a trap for the cat. Cute, but one wouldn't quite get the hoped-for result.

At long last, Tim left the house, but in his car, rather than on foot this time, which concerned her a bit. It was a deviation from the norm, and it meant that he could come back at any time, increasing her risk of exposure. He could just be too weary to walk. She imagined that his night had been restless after his impromptu nap on the dining room table, and the oddities that he had to have discovered when he awoke. Or, he could be planning something. Timmy wasn't dumb. She never could have put up with him if he had been dumb. Perhaps she should come back later. Sighing in frustration, and swatting absently at a persistent mosquito, who was trying to get a free meal from her neck, she decided to risk it. She was going in.

There were no unlocked doors or windows this time around, so she'd have to get creative. Delighted that she'd injected some fear and worry into the lives of Tim's neighbors, Susannah scouted out possible points of entry that would leave minimal trace if she had to force her way in.

"These two seem pretty typical," Susannah muttered to herself, thinking. "And if that's the case..." her eyes brightened and she slipped around to the side door, on a hunch.

She set her special pie on the humming air conditioner next to the door, then, standing on tiptoe, reaching the tips of her fingers to the top of the door frame, she touched exactly what she had expected – the key.

"Stupid," she chuckled.

If she'd had any sympathetic impulses at all, she may have felt almost sorry for the short-sightedness of the mother and daughter when it came to security, but she had no such qualms and was more than happy that getting in had been a piece of cake. Served them right for being so careless.

Going directly to the kitchen, Susannah set down the pie and proceeded to Marilyn's office.

Sitting down at the desk, she turned on the electric typewriter, hoping that it still worked. It hummed to life and she grabbed a piece of paper out of Marilyn's printer, rolling it into the outdated technology. Why Marilyn still had the antique was a mystery, but it suited her purpose, so she went ahead with her plan, tapping out a note from Tim. When she was finished, she turned off the typewriter, made certain that Marilyn's chair was in exactly the same spot it had been in when she entered the office, and took the note to the kitchen. Her hope was that Marilyn would think that Tiara had accepted the pie, and Tiara would think that Marilyn had. If they figured out that neither of them had brought it in, she'd just have to try again. The neighbors had been easy targets thus far, because apparently, they didn't have much of a tendency to overthink. Hopefully, Susannah's luck would hold out in that regard.

She left the house via the side door, locking it behind her. She'd keep the key, in case she needed to get in again, which she inevitably would, if they didn't fall for the pie ruse. She'd just shut the door, and was beginning to pull off her gloves when something bumped into her shin. Looking down, she saw a small cat. She'd noticed that Tim had dishes for food and water in his kitchen, and wondered if this creature belonged to him.

Reaching down with her gloved hand, she grabbed the cat by the scruff of the neck and held it up. The cat went motionless, staring at her with an unnatural calm.

"You're very mellow," Susannah observed. "It would make sense that you belonged to Tim," she nodded, turning the animal this way and that.

There was no collar and no identifying marks, like an ear tattoo, but she felt in her bones that this cat belonged to her husband.

"You're coming with me, little girl," she told the cat, who gave her a silent mew in return. "If you're his, he'll miss you, and if you're not, he'll be awfully freaked out when he eventually finds you in his house," she grinned wickedly.

Slipping through the trees on her usual route, still carrying the cat by the scruff, the sight that greeted her when she came out of the alley, near where she chose to park Angelica's car, took her breath away. She didn't park the car at the motel, not wanting anyone to see it in the same space day after day and get curious about it. The battered rust bucket was parked on the route that she took to get from Tim's neighborhood to the motel, so she could check on it every time she went back and forth. As she made her way out of the bushes at the end of the alley, she stopped short.

There was a police car parked behind Angelica's car, and one of Key West's finest stood behind it, speaking into the microphone attached to his vest. She couldn't read the expression of the cop, who wore mirrored sunglasses designed to inflame and intimidate, so she had to assume the worst.

"Shit," she growled, her teeth clenched in fury and frustration.

Taking care to not rattle the bushes unnecessarily, she backed up, keeping her eyes on the cop, who, so far, hadn't looked in her direction. Tim's cat let out a tiny mew, and she realized that she was gripping its scruff too hard. Forcibly relaxing her hand a bit, she considered just snapping the tiny neck and being done with it, but she didn't want to be that distracted at the moment. Thinking fast, she mapped out an alternate route to the motel. If the cops were sniffing around, they might start checking the less than reputable areas of town for Angelica, which could be disastrous. Had her body been found? Had a friend or family member reported her missing?

Susannah could no longer comfortably pass

herself off as Angelica, which just made life a bit more difficult. She hadn't used the dead girl's ID or credit cards since she left Chicago, but she'd been using her tablet and cell phone, and wondered if there was any way that the devices could be traced. Hating the thought of tossing away technology, Susannah knew that it was the only safe thing to do. She just had to get to them before the police did. She'd deleted her search history every time that she was finished using the tablet, but she wasn't naïve enough to believe that the forensics experts couldn't track it down. They'd see that she searched for her Timmy. They'd see that she'd researched Key West. They'd see research on funeral homes and decomposition of bodies in tropical climates, and they'd know. They'd know.

Moving fast, but more cautiously than normal, she skirted over a few blocks and approached the motel from behind, which meant slinking through a very sketchy neighborhood, with a tiny cat dangling from her fist. She hoped that she looked crazy enough to blend in with the locals and be left alone. She did, and she was.

Running from behind a clump of bushes, and taking cover behind a dumpster, Susannah crouched low and made her way around the side of the motel, where she saw another police car parked at the entrance to the grungy little lobby, which had film-covered windows and was protected by thick iron bars.

"Shit," she hissed again.

She needed to get to her room, but couldn't risk being seen. Everything of value that she had was in that room, including the tablet and phone, her killing tools, and her clothing. She'd stashed her souvenirs, the hair, tattoos and skin leaves of her most recent victims, under a large rock in a remote area of a rest stop, back on the mainland, so at least that evidence would remain hidden until she retrieved it. Part of her money was in her pants pocket, part of it was in Angelica's backpack in the motel room, and the rest she'd hidden under one of Tim's palmetto bushes.

A tickle of fear rose up in Susannah, along with another feeling that came out of nowhere. Turning to the side, she vomited, still holding Tim's ever-patient cat, the noxious mess spattering the asphalt and the building that she leaned against. After emptying her stomach, she continued retching for several seconds, her stomach twisting and contorting painfully.

"What the hell?" she whispered, wiping her

mouth with the back of her free hand and trying to catch her breath.

She must have accidentally had too much exposure to the laxatives that she'd gleefully shot into Tim's pie. If just that much exposure had done that to her, she could imagine what would happen to Marilyn and Tiara. In spite of the dire situation in which she currently found herself, that made her smile.

There was a chance that the police were at the shady motel for a reason which had nothing to do with Susannah. And there was also a chance that hell was freezing over. She wasn't going to gamble on the chance. She couldn't afford to. She mourned the loss of her knives, but there were several other problems that she had now. The presence of the knives fit her MO. The info on the computer and cell phone pointed directly to her. The rest of the belongings were from Angelica. It didn't take a rocket scientist to make those kinds of connections. They knew who and what Susannah was, what she was capable of, and soon...they would know where she was.

She was gripped by an urgency that was primal. She'd been taking a leisurely approach to inflicting harm and terror on Tim and his neighbors. Now, she'd have to make up her mind, finally, as to what she was going to do with her husband. It was time to act. First, she had to get somewhere safe so that she could think, and plan. Absently stroking the cat, Susannah's eyes darted back and forth as she plotted her next move. The smell of vomit rose to her nostrils and her stomach threatened to revolt again.

"I've gotta get out of here," she muttered, backing away from the mess.

She turned and slipped away, back into the neighborhood that she'd just come through. How and where she was going to hide while planning her final acts was a mystery, but she knew she had to get out of the area before police started searching for her in earnest.

CHAPTER TWENTY-FIVE

Tim woke with a start. The sun had begun to set, and his neck was stiff from the position he'd been in at the table. He'd had a horrific dream – that Susannah had found him – and upon waking from it, he felt as though she was there, with him. The dream seemed all too real, and the hair on the back of his neck stood up as he sat in his dining room chair, motionless and listening.

Maisie slinked against his ankle, making him jump, and he accidentally kicked the well-intentioned animal. She bore him no ill will however, promptly hopping up into his lap, purring, while he scratched between her ears, waiting for his heart rate to return to normal. Running a finger around the collar of his shirt, he felt unnaturally warm. That,

coupled with the fact that he'd been so uncharacter-
istically exhausted that he'd fallen asleep at the
table, made him wonder if he was coming down
with something. His skin was moist and the air
inside the house seemed overly humid, so he carried
the cat with him and went to check the thermostat,
just in case.

Standing slowly, aches and pains plaguing him,
he made his way through the living room, then
stopped. The blinds were closed, and he didn't
remember having closed them. He must've been
more tired than he thought. Continuing down the
hall, he flipped on the hall light so that he'd be able
to see the thermostat, which was on the wall right
next to the doorway of the guest room.

"No wonder it didn't come on," he frowned,
setting Maisie down gently in the hall.

The thermostat was set so that it wouldn't kick
on until the temperature in the house reached above
eighty degrees. It was currently a smothering
seventy-seven. This fall had been unseasonably
warm, and Tim wondered how he could have done
such a thing. He couldn't remember having touched
the thermostat in weeks. He clicked the setting down
several notches and the air conditioner kicked on,

sending a soothing hum through the house. When he glanced up, he saw that the blinds in the guest bedroom were open. He specifically always kept them closed, because the room faced the street and he didn't want anyone walking by to look in and see the empty room.

Tim's palms grew clammy as he stared at the blinds. Walking numbly to them, he twisted the rod and closed them tightly, then backed away, still staring. Maisie sat by his foot, licking her paw.

"Am I still dreaming?" he wondered aloud, passing a shaking hand over his brow.

If he was, it was the most eerily realistic dream he'd ever had. Tim walked across the hall, to his bedroom, like a man in a trance, fear gripping him like the icy hand of a specter. His master bedroom blinds, which he also never opened, feeling as though sunlight was an intrusion upon his cool dark box of a room, were open wide, the sunset painting pink stripes across the wall behind his bed. His heart sank, and he knew. Feeling as though he was being watched and was quite possibly about to confront his imminent demise, he moved toward his closet door which hung rudely open.

She was in there. He could feel it. Chills shook

him from head to toe, despite the lingering warmth and humidity in the house, and he fought to maintain his composure. He'd never let her see him tremble.

He stepped closer. And closer.

At any moment, she could jump out at him from the depths of his tidy, nearly empty closet. Hand shaking, he reached quickly into the closet, snapping on the light to reveal...nothing. Susannah wasn't in his closet. Nor was she in any of the others that he checked and closed, feeling like a complete idiot for allowing her to get to him like this.

Was it possible that he'd done it? Had he gone searching through his house for a phantom wife and forgotten to close the doors behind himself? His hands rose to his temples and he closed his eyes, squeezing his head in an attempt to clarify his racing thoughts.

Timothy Eckels wandered into his bathroom and stood over the sink, staring at his pale and haunted countenance. There were dark shadows under his eyes and his lips were parched and cracking. Was he ill? Or was his mind merely taking him places that he'd rather not go?

He looked down and saw his toothbrush lying beside the sink, on its side, bristles touching the solid surface of the vanity top. He knew with certainty that he hadn't done that. He would never do something so careless and disgusting. His toothbrush was always where it belonged, in the toothbrush holder, its bristles pristine. Snapping a strip of tissue off of the roll that was attached to the side of the vanity, and barely noticing that it had been put on backwards, he gingerly used it to pick up the toothbrush, and dropped it in the trash. God only knew what she'd done to it. He could be poisoned by it.

There was no uncertainty in him now. Susannah had violated his space, but at least she had left afterwards, rather than lying in wait for him.

He was alive, for now, and since he was still breathing, he was going to comfort himself in the only way he knew how...with a piece of pie. He'd made it from his grandmother's recipe and right now, that triple berry pie was his only tangible reminder that good people existed in the world. His grandmother had been one of them. Susannah had not. Feeling ill, but determined to get on with his life despite his wife's attempts to throw him off balance, he went to the kitchen and turned on the lights.

His pie was gone.

Not crushed, not missing a piece, not turned upside down in the sink...just...gone.

"She'd even deny me that simple pleasure," he sighed, reaching a hand to his hair and pulling it in frustration.

Wondering what other horrors might await him, he held his breath and pulled open the refrigerator. The contents appeared to be untouched, but when he slammed the door shut again, the fur-covered skull of one of his taxidermy projects fell down in front of him, rolling to a stop at his feet.

Tim resisted the urge to scream. As if sensing his angst, Maisie butted him in the ankle with her tiny head and he picked her up.

"I'm going to do something tonight that I rarely do, my feline friend," he whispered, holding the cat against his body and drawing comfort from her warmth. "I'm going to watch television. I need the mindless inanity of it, dear Maisie."

Making certain that all of his doors, windows and blinds were securely shut and locked down, he set the cat on the bed in his room and used the remote to turn on the only television set in the house, a small flat-screen that rested atop his dresser. Flipping through channels, he saw a news-cast that made his heart stop. He sat straight up in bed, his eyes glued to the screen and turned up the volume. The picture was of a young woman who strongly resembled Susannah, but with more delicate features and short, mahogany-toned hair. Apparently, police had found a car belonging to the young woman in question, who had disappeared from a town in Iowa.

Perhaps this had been the woman he'd seen across the street from the pie shop. He'd been a bit ridiculous lately, now that he thought about it. His mind conjuring Susannah around every corner. But the toothbrush...and leaving the closet doors open... he would never have done those things, even when he was dog-tired. There had to be some other explanation, and his mind had automatically leapt to Susannah. Maybe Marilyn from next door had come in looking for something. Maybe there had been a burglar who didn't find any of Tim's meager belongings to his liking. Or a realtor who thought the house was still for rent. Studying the photo on the television, he could see definite differences between the girl in the picture and Susannah. Did she even resemble her at all? Or was he merely looking for a resemblance?

Tim finally decided that worrying would get him nowhere, so he'd just forget about the strange events that had happened at his house. He needed to move on with his life and constantly brooding over his wife certainly wasn't going to help him do that.

And he was still going to buy another toothbrush.

CHAPTER TWENTY-SIX

It had been a long day, and Marilyn was bushed. She'd gotten home about half an hour after Tiara, and found her daughter sitting at the kitchen table eating a massive slice of berry pie.

"I cut you a slice too," Tiara said with her mouth full, pointing a fork at another plate with pie on it, in front of the chair across from her.

"Mmm...that looks amazing," Marilyn's mouth watered. "But you forgot something."

"Dinner?" Tiara grinned. "I figured pie was a nice healthy alternative for dinner," she joked.

"Well, of course it is," Marilyn chuckled. "What you forgot is the ice cream."

She went to the freezer and pulled out a tub of rich, creamy vanilla bean, and scooped a generous portion out for each of them. Tiara had already eaten several bites of pie, but took a heaping helping of the ice cream anyway.

The two of them sat in relative silence, enjoying the treat, occasionally uttering sounds of contentment. After they'd finished, they both sat in their chairs feeling full and happy.

"Are you going to yoga in the morning?" Marilyn asked Tiara, scrolling through her phone to check her calendar.

"Of course," Tiara grinned, scraping her fork around her plate to get every last drop of pie and ice cream that still lingered there.

"I've gotta tell you, honey...I'm not really feeling good about your interest in the instructor," her mother confessed, picking up both of their plates and taking them to the dishwasher.

"And why might that be?" Tiara was immediately defensive.

"Well, let's see...he's older than you, he's cocky, he's a silver-tongued devil who knows how to tell a girl what she wants to hear..." Marilyn ticked off points on her fingers.

"Oh, please, Motherrrr..." Tiara rolled her eyes. "You don't even..."

Her words cut off abruptly. Her hands clutched at her stomach and her face went white as she jumped up from the table and ran to the bathroom.

"Ti?" Marilyn knocked lightly on the bathroom door, hearing some decidedly unpleasant sounds coming from within. "Are you okay?"

"Go away," Tiara moaned.

"Fine," Marilyn sighed, shaking her head.

She went back to the kitchen and began flipping through the mail, a funny feeling in her stomach. Passing it off as merely being the result of having eaten the rich, sugary, pie and ice cream too quickly, she realized suddenly that Tiara had been in the bathroom for quite some time.

"Honey, are you okay in there?" she stood at the door knocking again. "I'm worried about you."

A cramp struck her just then, and she nearly doubled over.

"No, I'm not okay," Tiara admitted weakly. "There's something really wrong with my stomach, Mom," she groaned, sounding scared.

"Oh god," Marilyn gasped. "I'll be right back."

She ran down the hall to her own bathroom, barely making it in time, as her bowels proceeded to explode in watery ruin. Sitting on the toilet, between painful spasms, she texted her daughter, whom she knew would have her phone with her.

"*Where did you buy that pie?*"

"*I didn't buy it,*" was Tiara's reply. "*The neighbor brought it over, there's a note. Didn't he give it to you...?*"

"*No.*"

Marilyn was shaking, not with anger at the neighbor, though that was definitely a factor, but because of the painful horror that her body was going through at the moment, and she felt helpless knowing that Tiara was enduring the same thing.

"*The bathroom is a mess,*" Tiara texted, nearly half an hour later. "*I had to throw up, but I couldn't get off of the toilet, and now my body keeps trying to throw up, even though I'm empty. It hurts so bad.*"

"*Hang on, honey. I'm going to get us some help,*" Marilyn replied, having just filled her bathroom wastebasket for the same reason.

Something was dramatically wrong with the two of them, and, as embarrassing as it might be, she had to call the man whom she'd only recently begun seeing, Detective Bernard "Cort" Cortland. He could call an ambulance for her and Tiara, instructing them to be discreet so that the neighbors wouldn't be standing out in their driveways rubbernecking, and he could also go next door and arrest their odd and vindictive neighbor, Timothy Eckels. Why would the strange little man have done such a thing? Just because she hadn't hired him? That was just plain crazy, and the thought that a crazy man had moved in next door was not something that she was prepared to put up with.

After dark, Susannah had stopped wandering around town, looking for a resting place, and had returned to her nest among the bushes on Tim's street, where she could observe his house and Marilyn's. She'd just settled in when an unmarked police car, followed by an ambulance, pulled up in front of Marilyn's house. Apparently, they had eaten the pie. Susannah bit back a sinister giggle.

She watched the EMT's load the women into the ambulance with barely concealed glee, but her elation turned to a bit of concern when the ambulance left and the detective who'd driven the unmarked went over and banged on Timmy's door. That wasn't part of the plan. She hadn't wanted him to get arrested, she'd only wanted to stir up some interesting drama between him and his obnoxious neighbors. If her husband went to jail, she'd neither be able to torment him, nor join forces with him. The decision would be taken out of her hands, and she definitely didn't like that. Not one bit.

CHAPTER TWENTY-SEVEN

Timothy Eckels had never had occasion to see the inside of a police station before, even when it had been discovered that his wife was a serial killer. The police had come to him and questioned him in the privacy of his own home. It was quite a fascinating experience being among those who had broken the law, alongside those who were tasked with enforcing it. The hostile dregs of society were being held captive by those who suspected them, rightly or wrongly, of breaking their social contract. It seemed to Tim that there must surely be a better way of handling disputes between people, but what did he know?

He was led down dull beige corridors which smelled of old coffee and body odor, to an interrogation room, where he felt as though the detective expected him to be overwhelmed or intimidated, but his reality was quite the opposite. He actually felt safe. Susannah couldn't get to him in here. People like her were treated very carefully. Although, the last time that these crusading mortals had tried to contain her, they had failed, miserably.

"Anything you want to tell me, Eckels?" the detective asked casually, his eyes sharp, missing nothing.

"No," Tim answered simply.

One could not be misunderstood if one did not elaborate.

"You bake pies," Cort surprised him by saying.

"Yes," Tim agreed, holding fast to the concept that the less said, the better.

"You gave your neighbors a pie," another casual statement.

Tim frowned, confused. He hadn't given Marilyn and Tiara a pie for quite some time. It had been weeks.

"It was a special pie, wasn't it, Eckels?" Cort persisted, his tone growing harder.

"I'm sorry, I don't understand..." Tim began.

"Don't give me that, Eckels. What were you

hoping to accomplish with that? You know, I could probably escalate this from felony assault to attempted murder if you don't cooperate," the detective leaned forward, getting close enough that Tim could smell the faint trace of aftershave that remained on his skin after a long day.

Tim stared at him, utterly befuddled. He pushed his heavy glasses up onto the bridge of his nose with one finger.

"I have no idea what you're talking about," he shook his head. "Pies and assault and murder...it makes no sense."

"Don't play dumb with me, Eckels. I know who you are. I know why you came to Florida, and I don't think it's a coincidence that someone from your neighborhood was found in his backyard with his eyes, fingers and mouth glued shut, just like they would be in a mortuary. Your fingerprints are all over that one, buddy," Cort accused.

Tim said nothing. How could the bodybuilder have been found in his backyard? Tim had left him at the docks and had not expected him to return. He would never kill another human being, but what the thugs with whom he'd left the guy might do, was not his problem.

"But that's not why we're here right now," the detective continued. "I wanna know why you did this terrible thing to your neighbors. Those ladies have never been anything but nice to you."

"I don't know what you're talking about," Tim said honestly.

Sure, he'd done his work on the bodybuilder, but he'd done nothing to Marilyn or Tiara. He assumed that they were the neighbors to whom the detective was referring. Cortland opened a file folder and tossed a piece of paper, secured in an evidence bag, onto the table between them.

"This is what I'm talking about. Read it, but don't even think about opening the bag," he warned.

Sweets for the sweet. Hope you're feeling better, Tiara. Here's a token of my esteem. Please enjoy it as a gesture of community and friendship. No hard feelings ~ Timothy Eckels

Tim read the typewritten words once, then twice, then again. When he looked up at the detective, he stared, mouth agape.

"Where did you get this?" he asked hoarsely.

"From Marilyn's kitchen counter top. It was sitting right next to the pie that sent both her and Tiara to the hospital this evening," the detective ground out, a vein on his forehead pulsing.

"I didn't do this," Tim protested, eyes going wide. "I mean, it sounds like the way that I speak. If I were going to make a gesture like this, I'd probably phrase it in a similar manner, but reaching out to people, even nice people, in this way, is simply not something that I do," he shook his head. "I keep to myself. I don't...give people things...or even talk to them if they don't talk to me first."

"So, you hate people?" Cortland challenged.

"No, they frighten me. I'm not well-versed in societal norms. I'm rather awkward, so people generally find it uncomfortable to be in my presence," Tim shrugged.

"And you resent that," the detective accused. It wasn't a question.

"No, I understand it. I wouldn't want to keep company with someone like myself either. I've grown accustomed to being alone."

"Especially after your wife turned out to be a serial killer, huh?" the detective smirked.

Tim said nothing. Speaking of Susannah always made him uncomfortable. It wasn't fair that her stains had bled onto him...so to speak.

"You left Minnesota pretty quickly when your wife was arrested. Why was that?" Cortland's eyes were piercing.

"Because it was a small town. My business was finished because of what she did. People looked at me funny. Whispered about me, crossed the street to avoid me. I didn't want to live that way," Tim sighed. "And, when I heard that she escaped, I feared for my life."

Susannah's misdeeds haunted him still, just as he'd suspected they would.

"You only gave your realtor a post office box, rather than an address. Why is that?" the detective asked.

"I didn't want her to find me," Tim mumbled.

"You didn't want who to find you?"

"My wife."

Tim couldn't bring himself to say her name to another person.

"Yet you didn't divorce her."

"I didn't think about it. I just wanted to be somewhere safe, where she couldn't find me."

"Where is your wife now, Mr. Eckels?" Cortland asked, his voice low.

Tim found himself at a crossroads. There was every chance that, if he told the truth and admitted his suspicions about Susannah's whereabouts, it would sound like he was just using her as an excuse to cover his own foul deeds. They wouldn't believe him.

Or, they might believe him and would ask him what evidence he had to back up his assertions. He had none. If Susannah had done the things in his house, she would be smart enough to wear gloves and protect her hair and skin so that there'd be no trace evidence in his home.

Timothy Eckels was a man trapped between a bad choice and a worse one.

"My cat is missing," he remembered suddenly.

Maisie had been gone all day. He'd called her and called her, but she'd never come back in after he let her out this morning. She'd stayed with him all night, while he'd slept with the television on, but hadn't returned during the day.

Detective Cortland let out an explosive, frustrated exhalation.

"I don't see how that's relevant."

The fact that Susannah had assaulted Marilyn and Tiara made Tim sad and embarrassed. The thought that she had harmed even one silky hair on Maisie's petite head filled him with impotent rage. He'd tear her limb from limb if she'd harmed his pet. It was time to throw caution to the wind and throw Susannah directly under the bus.

"She's been stalking me," he admitted, feeling a huge weight lifting from his soul. "It wouldn't be too much of a stretch to think that she may have been jealous of my relationship with Tiara."

"Relationship?" a muscle in the detective's jaw flexed and Tim could feel fury radiating from him in waves.

"Not like that," he assured the detective with a tired wave of his hand. "We were friends, such as it were. She'd come over sometimes and talk to me and have pie and tea. She was polite."

"Did her mother know about this?" Cort raised an eyebrow.

"I think so. She came over once and found her there. I think she was surprised that we weren't conducting ritual sacrifices or something," Tim's attempt at a joke fell flat in the face of the detective's silence.

Detective Bernard Cortland stared at Tim hard, and for a long time. Tim's gaze wasn't defiant, but it never wavered. Tim squirmed in his chair, wondering if he would end up spending some time in a smelly cell with a chain-smoker named Bubba. Finally, the detective seemed to reach a decision and spoke.

"What makes you think it's your wife who's

stalking you?" he asked, seeming to actually take Tim seriously.

"Either she's stalking me, or I have lost my mind entirely," Tim admitted.

Feeling as though he'd been given a gift, he told the detective everything.

CHAPTER TWENTY-EIGHT

Susannah had seen another newscast. She didn't know how, but the police had figured it out. They knew that she had killed Angelica for her identity, and they knew that she was in Key West. After watching the story on a television in a crowded diner, she had ducked out, taking her leftover onion rings with her.

Sitting with her back against a pylon, on the rocks underneath the docks where she'd found Tim and the bodybuilder, she munched the rest of her dinner, her mind working at a fevered pace. They knew about her now. They were looking for her. Which meant she had to leave, with or without her Timmy. She still didn't know whether or not she wanted to kill him eventually, but right now, oddly, she yearned to simply lie in bed, with his body warm next to hers.

Her sentimentality disgusted her, particularly when she began to cry. Susannah never cried, yet here she sat, giant ugly sobs braying from her like an ass with a burr under its saddle. She cried so hard, and for so long, that she ended up gagging, her recently-consumed dinner landing on the rocks beside the pylon. Not knowing where to go she wandered in the darkness. She needed to get as far away from Florida as possible, but there was something she had to do first.

Susannah had no idea how she looked as she made her way through the dark streets of the shuttered town. More pitiful than terrifying, her faux tourist clothing dirty, rumpled and loose from recent weight loss, she appeared to be homeless and forlorn. The murderous gleam which usually darkened her gaze had dimmed a bit, leaving her looking unhinged, but in a sad sort of way rather than a dangerous one.

As she walked, however, muttering to herself and reviewing events of the past several days, the killing fire began to rekindle in the depths of her dark heart.

"He told them," she growled under her breath,

her steps quickening. "He's the only one who knows me. He sold me out," her feet stamped harder and faster on the pavement as she instinctively avoided her usual routes.

Susannah wasn't even thinking about where she was going. Her drive to right what had been wronged in her world propelled her body forward. She traveled on instinct and fury. There was no doubt in her mind now. Timothy Eckels had played the wrong card and lost the game. There would be no second chance for him. No opportunity for an unholy alliance of murder and mayhem with his mate. He'd crossed the line and had betrayed her, probably in an attempt to save his own pathetic skin. He was going to die, and it would be a long, slow, painful death. Every torture method that she'd ever wanted to try, she'd use on Tim. She just had to get to him before he did the cowardly thing again, and fled.

By the time she neared Tim's quiet neighborhood, where normal people slept, unaware of the malignant presence moving among them, she was practically running, her normally controlled and precise breathing huffing out of her in harsh gasps of anger and exertion. When Tim's simple home loomed into view, she slowed, becoming aware of her potential exposure. She had a job to do, she couldn't afford to get caught. Not here, not now, not when she was this close to finishing the job.

She'd found her husband, she'd allowed herself to fantasize about his possible transition to the dark side, and she'd gotten screwed, unfortunately figuratively rather than literally. Right now, however, her rage burned hotter than her libido, and her goal was unambiguous. Tim had to suffer, and writhe, and scream, and die.

Standing among the saw-bladed palmettos across the street, she scanned the area for any sign of police presence, but saw nothing. There was no breeze, no movement. Only the sound of cars in the distance marred the perfect silence of the night. Susannah had brought no weapons with her. Not only had there not been time to procure her instruments of choice, but she thought it would be much more poetic if she flayed him alive with the same knives that his beloved grandmother had used to slice fruit for her pies. This particular killing was to be her crown jewel, she planned to make everything about it a supreme experience for her.

Slipping quickly across the street, staying in the shadows as much as possible, Susannah decided to try the easiest possible route first. Slinking onto the front porch, where the light was oddly not turned on, she grasped the door knob and turned. There were no gloves on her hands this time. She wanted them to know who had done the thing that would be done here tonight, in this simple house in this quiet neighborhood. It wouldn't be right to leave Timothy Eckels' death to speculation. She was claiming it, brazenly displaying her work. Her name would strike fear into the hearts of his neighbors and make them wonder if they were next. While they were busy buying alarm systems, canine protection and ammunition, she would have moved on, leaving a trail of her husband's blood behind her. Too bad she couldn't claim his life insurance payout. She was the beneficiary on the document, after all.

Much to Susannah's astonishment, the door opened, swinging inward, to total darkness. That gave her pause. Was this a game? Was Tim trying to toy with her? The thought made her seethe. Stepping inside, she slammed the door behind her and locked it, wanting to startle him, wanting to announce her presence, wanting to make him come crawling. Crouching low, she quickly searched every room, finally determining that Tim wasn't home. Had he been so scared that he was spending the night in a hotel? Doubtful. Tim hated the thought of sleeping in a bed that had borne the weight of multitudes of strangers.

Taking a chance, she flipped on the light in the kitchen. Sitting on the counter was the business card of Detective Bernard Cortland. That's where Tim the Coward was. He'd gone to give a statement. A white-hot fury rose within her. She was so ready to inflict fatal harm on her husband that she ached with the want of it. And now he'd denied her. Again.

Tearing the card into tiny pieces, Susannah threw them into the garbage disposal and raided Tim's drawers to stock up on knives. She had a feeling that she'd need them, and soon. Frustrated to no end, she decided to arm herself and wait him out. She'd simply lurk in the bushes next to his house so that she'd be alerted the moment that he came home.

Before she left the house, she went into his master bathroom. She knew that his toiletries would be kept in the top right-hand drawer of the vanity. Timothy Eckels was a creature of habit, and he'd always kept them there, no matter where he'd lived. Feeling strangely conflicted, she went into the bathroom and slowly opened the drawer. Staring down at Tim's things – his razor, his plastic box of dental floss, a box of bandages, she pulled a small object out of her pocket.

Touching the object deliberately, so that her fingerprints would be all over it, she dropped it into the drawer with a shuddering breath, then pushed the drawer closed, her fingers lingering briefly on the wood front of it. Shaking herself mentally, she turned off the bathroom light and slipped back out the front door, going immediately to her hiding spot.

Susannah yawned and rolled her head from side to side to relieve her stiff, tense, neck muscles, then froze. Something had rustled in the bushes behind her. Had she imagined it? She couldn't hear very well when her mouth was opened wide in the yawn. Still crouched in the bushes, she waited, not moving.

A low sound made the hairs at the base of her skull stand up and sent shivers running down her spine. She heard the sound again, closer this time and more constant. A growl. One that sounded like it was coming from a not-so-friendly canine.

"I don't want to kill an animal," Susannah whispered, her teeth clenched.

Yet another distraction. She couldn't afford to make too many movements, possibly giving away her position, and she didn't want to risk the animal making a pained yelp and calling attention to her.

The growling got closer, and as she weighed the possibilities of how she should handle the situation, she felt the cold sensation of metal on the back of her neck.

The dog advanced, and she saw that it was an aging golden retriever. She nearly laughed with relief, but then, there was the small matter of potentially being shot. The gunman wasn't a cop, he would have announced himself immediately, and given her a command. With a minor obstacle in front of her, and a pretty major one behind, she decided to play it smart, rather than trying to bring matters to a physical showdown. She didn't yet know what she was dealing with. Her childhood days on the farm would come in handy if she had to take out the dog. She knew right where to slice, but she had to know if the man at her back was tall or short, stocky or spare, and how young, old or fit he was.

How did she know that it was a man? A woman would have started talking immediately. It was something she found utterly distasteful about her fellow gender members. Talk, talk, talk.

"Don't move," the man finally said.

Susannah heard the tremor in his voice and was encouraged. It also sounded like he was older, another plus.

"Don't shoot," she pleaded, making her voice sound as weak and vulnerable as she could muster.

The man took the gun from the base of her neck.

"Stand up and turn around," he ordered.

Susannah took a deep breath and smelled a scent with which she was unfortunately familiar. The man was overweight. She knew it without seeing him, because she could pick up on the scent that occurs only between folds of human flesh lying thickly upon itself. For a specific art project, she'd wanted to harvest skin that had multiple stretch marks, thinking that the stripes of it would add texture to her piece. She'd had a domineering asshole of a boss at the time, who happened to be obese. He tried to feel her up during food prep one day, and she'd dispatched of him that night. He had smelled like that...of flesh and folds and stripes.

It was difficult not to smile as she turned around. Chances are, if he was fat, he'd also be slow, and would have no stamina in a physical altercation. She'd play it cool as long as she could, but she knew with certainty that she'd be sending this gunslinger to the hereafter in short order, and she needed to get on with it before Tim came home.

Susannah turned and found that her assumption was correct. The thickly bearded man was not merely obese, he looked to be morbidly obese. She'd have no trouble dispatching with the meatball, and once she did, his dog would go to him rather than turning on her. Perfect.

"What are you doing out here?" he demanded, his pistol dipping and rising as he held it pointed at her.

His arms were that shaky. The weight of the gun had his muscles burning with effort. This could be fun.

"I'm sorry, I'm homeless and I just needed a place to rest. I was just passing through. I wasn't hurting anything," Susannah kept her voice plaintive, pretending to be scared. "I don't like guns, though. Could you put that down, please? I'll just leave. I'm sorry," she physically made her lower lip quiver.

She hadn't lied entirely. She didn't like guns. They were far too brutish and impersonal. To get up close and personal with death, one needed a blade. The contrast of deep, rich, red blood on a shiny blade was a thing of beauty.

"Are you a policeman?" she asked, wide-eyed, appealing to Tubby's ego.

He slowly lowered the gun and shook his head.

"Neighborhood watch, ma'am," he said grimly, with as much authority as he could summon.

"Oh, sure," Susannah nodded, laughter threatening to bubble up and out of her. "They're lucky to have you. I'll just be going now, if you don't mind."

In her peripheral vision, she noted that the golden retriever had gotten bored and was sniffing around in the bushes.

"I do mind," he thundered, bringing the gun back up and taking a stance, feet shoulder width apart. "There have been cops all over this neighborhood the last couple of days. I'm not just gonna let you walk out of here," he warned.

Susannah took in his tough guy posture and mentally shook her head. He might as well have been wearing a neon sign that said, 'Hey, I'm exposed. Kick me in the crotch and escape.'

"It didn't have to be this way," she told him ruefully.

He frowned, baffled.

"What are you talk..."

He didn't get to finish his question. Susannah lunged forward, knocking the gun to the side with one hand, and landing a knee squarely between his legs before he could even react. Adrenaline flowing in a most glorious way, she was terribly sad that she wouldn't be able to take the time to enjoy her kill. The self-appointed guardian of the neighborhood hit the deck after uttering a strangled cry, clutching his private parts. She was surprised that he could reach them under his considerable belly. He rolled to the side, his mouth a whitened rictus of pain. As predicted, when his owner hit the deck, the dog trotted over, whimpering and sniffing about his head and face.

Susannah couldn't even take the time to flip him over so that she could look into his eyes as he died. She pulled one of Tim's butcher knives out of her stash, which she'd kept wrapped in a towel nearby – she'd have to pick up another backpack soon – and sliced his throat with professional precision, his blood glurting out in thick jets that she imagined were composed of equal parts blood and fat.

"Sorry, dog," she said absently, wiping the knife on the man's shirt as his dog whined and licked at the wound, it's muzzle getting saturated in blood.

A siren sounded in the distance, and Susannah knew that it was time to go. As much as she might want to, she couldn't wait around to kill Tim. There were very few means of getting off of the island, and as the investigation intensified, it would be more and more difficult, potentially involving more and more killing. At least this death had taken a bit of the edge off. She was more than prepared to kill whoever she needed to in order to make her way back to the mainland, but for now, she was done. It was time to move on.

When Tim returned from the police station, drained and weary, but content that they had at least believed him enough to do more investigation, he was delighted to see that Maisie had returned. She twined back and forth between his feet as he unlocked his front door. Police were combing the area in case Susannah tried to get to him, since her behavior seemed to be escalating.

Tim had come to a decision. He'd put Marilyn and Tiara in danger, just by being there. This was their home, for him it had merely been a stepping stone – a means to get away from his homicidal mate. Since she'd found him, they were no longer safe, nor was he. The answer was simple, he had to move. He liked the beach, so he'd try to stay in the state of Florida, but he needed to keep moving for a while before he settled in somewhere.

He knew he wouldn't be able to sleep tonight, despite his exhaustion, so he began packing up his meager belongings. He'd leave before dawn, if he could get ready in time, not willing to spend even another day presenting a danger to his neighbors.

By the time he got to the bathroom, where all of his toiletries were kept in a single drawer, he was so tired that he could barely see straight, yet he kept going. What he found in the bathroom not only made him snap fully awake, but it kept him awake for many nights, and haunted him during the day. Opening the drawer, his toiletry case in hand, he found an object that he didn't recognize at first, but when he picked it up and examined it more closely, there was no mistaking it.

A plastic stick, with a clear plastic window on one end and a cap on the other. Two distinct pink lines glaring up at him through the window, taunting him, mocking him. A positive result that made for very negative circumstances. Susannah was pregnant.

"Dear god," he whispered, and fell to the floor.

AUTHOR'S NOTE

I sincerely hope that you enjoyed reading The Killing Girl as much as I enjoyed writing it. Thanks so much for spending time with another S. Prescott Thriller. I would love it if you'd be so kind as to leave a review to let me know how much you liked (or disliked) the book. Reader feedback is very important to me, and my hope is that you enjoyed it so much that you'd want to comment on it.

The Killing Girl can be enjoyed fully as a stand alone. If you'd like to learn more about Susannah and Tim's past, you'll want to pick up the prequel, The Quiet Type, at your favorite retailer.

The Quiet Type

If you'd like to be among the first to be notified about the release of spine-tingling new Thrillers, and receive a newsletter and information about free gifts, prizes and contests, just shoot an email to the address below.

Also – feel free to share your impressions of the book. S. Prescott Thrillers takes reader feedback very seriously – we couldn't do what we do, if it wasn't for you! Thanks for reading!

summer.prescott.thrillers@gmail.com

Follow Me On Twitter

Follow Me On Instagram

CPSIA information can be obtained
at www.ICGtesting.com
Printed in the USA
LVHW021603020820
662192LV00002B/166

9 781799 020462